MARTHA *and* MARY

Also by Patty Froese Ntihemuka:
The Woman at the Well

To order,
call
1-800-765-6955.

Visit us at
www.AutumnHousePublishing.com
for information on other Autumn House® products.

MARTHA and MARY

Saving the Sisters From Bethany

PATTY FROESE NTIHEMUKA

Autumn House® Publishing
www.autumnhousepublishing.com
A Division of **REVIEW AND HERALD® PUBLISHING**
Since 1861

Published by Autumn House® Publishing, a division of Review and Herald® Publishing, Hagerstown, MD 21741-1119

The author assumes full responsibility for the accuracy of all facts and quotations as cited in this book.

Bible texts in this book are from the *Holy Bible, New International Version.* Copyright © 1973, 1978, 1984, International Bible Society. Used by permission of Zondervan Bible Publishers.

This book was
Edited by Gerald Wheeler
Designed by Ron J. Pride
Interior designed by Heather Rogers
Cover artwork is *At Jesus' Feet,* by artist Nathan Greene. Copyright © 2003, Nathan Greene. All rights reserved. For more information on the complete line of art by Nathan Greene, call 1-800-487-4278 or visit www.hartclassics.com.
Typeset: Bembo 12/14.75

PRINTED IN U.S.A.

12 11 10 09 08   5 4 3 2 1

Library of Congress Cataloging-in-Publication Data
Ntihemuka, Patty Froese, 1978-   .
  Martha and Mary : saving the sisters from Bethany / Patty Froese Ntihemuka.
    p. cm.
  1. Martha, Saint—Fiction. 2. Mary, of Bethany, Saint—Fiction. 3. Christian women saints—Fiction. 4. Bible. N.T.—History of Biblical events—Fiction. 5. Women in the Bible—Fiction. I. Title.

PR9199.4.N825M37 2008
  813'.6—dc22
                              2007034542

ISBN 978-0-8127-0471-6

DEDICATION

To my husband, Jean,

with all my love

CHAPTER 1

"Whatever you bind on earth will be bound in heaven, and whatever you loose on earth will be loosed in heaven."

He is well established. His family weaves fine-quality fabrics. All regard him as a fair bargainer and a man who measures honestly."

Martha let her eyes fall to her lap, absently exploring the quality of her own tunic. It was not expertly woven, and she could see places where snags had been covered over during the weaving process. The fabric fell imperfectly, though she wasn't one to complain. But a husband who could provide her with quality clothing—that was something to consider.

She sat cross-legged on a mat she had woven herself in the sitting area of their humble home. Her brother had ceremoniously led her here, then sat, choosing his words carefully for several silent moments before speaking. The walls had been plastered by an adequate craftsman and whitewashed, then painted in a golden brown color that reminded Martha of a sunrise. Several tapestries adorned the walls, and she regarded one silently as she thought—her eyes following the zigzagged lines of red and blue as her mind took in the information. The scent of freshly baked bread floated across the room to her, and she mentally began to tally the work that still needed doing. This room needed to be swept. The dust and grit from the blowing sand outside always worked its way in. Even now she could see the dust settling. Why did her mind always have to run along the most mundane paths whenever she faced something momentous?

"He is kind. No one has ever known him to beat his first wife. She is always dressed well, and her kin tell that she is treated fairly. I've looked into that."

"I know you would," Martha said, shifting her gaze to meet her brother's concerned eyes.

"She is well fed and has anything she wants." His voice was steady, but his expression betrayed some worry. Men never were very good at masking their feelings.

"However, as second wife, would I be treated as fairly as his first wife?" Martha asked pragmatically.

"He hasn't cheated anyone yet," her brother said slowly. "I don't imagine he would start with you. I would take care of the contract and make sure you got your due."

"Why is he acquiring a second wife?"

"For an heir. You have a few more good years for children."

Martha nodded. While she would be the second wife, she would also, with God's blessing, be the mother of his children. His first wife might be his love, but his second wife would allow his name to continue. She would have a secure enough position. The man was taking a chance, however, that she would be able to have children. Already 27—what if she was also barren? What if conceiving was not easy for her? He would have two barren women on his hands. One he loved, and one he had acquired for the purpose of children but who had failed him.

"It is a good proposition . . ." he said slowly. "Considering . . ."

She knew what he meant by that. Considering her age. Considering her appearance. Considering that no other men had been eager to make her theirs. *It's a good proposition considering that no one else seems to want me,* she thought with less bitterness than acceptance.

It was strange how a woman could get passed over. It happened, however. Perhaps there were enough girls born in a village, or even too many. Perhaps it was her looks—not quite as fresh and appealing as the other women. Or perhaps it was the name she carried—Martha, sister of Lazarus, as the villagers knew her—Martha bath Moseh, more formally. Unfortunately, another "sister of Lazarus" had a reputation that was hard to ignore. There was another daughter of Moseh, whom people talked about behind their hands. Or sometimes not behind their hands at all. Mary was not a secret.

"You've met him, I'm sure," Lazarus went on. "His name is Jebuseh. He looks well for his age. Strong and tall."

"I remember dreaming of my husband when I was a girl," Martha said, her eyes misting with unshed tears. Lazarus shifted uncomfortably. "I dreamed that a man would desire me, even if it was on the day of our wedding and the first time he had laid eyes on me. We would have a whole houseful of babies, and I would be enough for him. I never dreamed to be the second."

"Perhaps I haven't done as well by you as I should have," her brother said quietly. "When father died, I promised I would provide for both of you."

"Ah, Lazarus." Martha put a hand on his knee and shook her head. It had been the same since they were children. She had been the logical one, while Lazarus had always felt guilty about something that was not his fault. And Mary . . . she had been something different altogether.

"Stop beating yourself up for finding yourself a wife, brother," Martha said, allowing a smile to play at her lips. "Would you have stayed single and alone until a man decided to take me? Don't be ridiculous!"

"If I had put more attention into your matches—"

"You did, Lazarus," she said, cutting him short. "Some things are beyond even your best intentions."

"I know you don't want to be second."

"I don't. However, it is better than being unmarried, is it not?"

The question hung in the air unanswered. She felt like repeating it—forcing a response from him. But his thoughts seemed to be elsewhere.

"Rachel approved of him, as well," Lazarus said tentatively.

"She would."

"Rachel loves you, you know." His voice had a touch of reproach. "She wants you to have a home of your own."

"I didn't mean anything by it," Martha replied, trying to brush it aside. "Only words."

"And children of your own! Respect of the community!"

"You don't need to remind me of what I do not have," she replied with some heat. "Rachel was fortunate to marry young. Perhaps she was more than fortunate. Perhaps it was her beauty, or her family. I have neither."

The words stung. Martha could see it the moment they left her lips. Her brother flinched visibly.

"I'm sorry your family does not command the kind of respect you would like," he said in a low voice. "Perhaps if I was a more successful merchant, or more known for my hospitality . . ."

"I don't insult you, Lazarus," she said with a sigh. "You know perfectly well whom I speak of."

"She is my sister too."

"But she did not hinder your marriage opportunities."

Perhaps Mary had not affected Martha's marriage chances, either. That was the weight that pressed down on her heart. Perhaps it was not Mary's fault, after all. Perhaps Martha's advanced age, being nearly at her twenty-seventh year, and her unmarried situation were because of something else, something more personal. Perhaps she was simply undesirable.

"Do you want time to think about this . . . opportunity?" Lazarus said after Martha had not spoken for several moments.

"No."

"You don't want him."

"No, I meant that I do not want more time to think."

"What shall I tell Jebuseh?"

"That, God willing, I will submit to the arrangements and be his wife."

It was a strange time for the family. Life had not unfolded the way anyone had hoped or planned. Martha, Lazarus, and Mary had lost their parents when Lazarus was only 14. Martha had been 16 at the time, and Mary 15. She'd been marriageable then, at least in her father's eyes. When he made Lazarus promise to find husbands for his daughters, Moseh must have believed that, with Simon's help, it would only be a matter of months before both his girls joined the homes of their husbands' families.

By far Martha had been the most prepared of the three for the death of their parents. She was the most logical and reliable. But Lazarus was the male, and he would shoulder the responsibilities of the family. He would live with the blame for his sisters' unmarried status.

So instead of joining a husband's family, Martha stayed with her own to face the uncertain times. Sickness was like that. The closest family members never wanted to admit the severity of the illness. The more distantly related family members coldly discussed who would benefit from the death. But the illness was there—palpable like an extra guest no one wanted to visit. Sickness was the extra guest that everyone was expecting to do something impolite and unwelcome.

While Martha tried to accustom herself to the idea of marrying a much older man and being a second wife, her uncle lay on what was likely his deathbed. Uncle Simon. He had been like a father to them after their own father's death. Lazarus hadn't been strong enough or old enough to be a father to his older sisters. Uncle Simon, however, had been there.

But then Uncle Simon had always been there. Extended family was a part of every person's life. Cousins, aunts and uncles, brothers and sisters, in-laws, nieces and nephews . . . it was a complicated web of obligation and responsibility. As brother of the deceased, it was Simon's duty to protect the dead man's family. Whether he wanted to or not, it was expected, and the community would watch him pointedly until he fulfilled his obligation. So like every other family member, Uncle Simon had always been an integral part of Martha's life. But the details of their carefully balanced relationship remained a secret from everyone. Well, everyone, that is, but Mary.

Uncle Simon had been sick for some time. His house— known for being one of the most wealthy in the village—had the smell of illness in it . . . that sour stench of sweat and dry mouth. His living area was expertly plastered and painted in bright colors. The cooking area in the courtyard was spacious, and the upper sleeping chamber was comfortable and separated off by thick, high quality curtains. Such a home was something to be envied, except for that smell of sickness that pervaded every crevice. The family had thought some years ago that he would die, but he had pulled through by a miracle. Now he was ill again, but a miracle seemed far in coming. The old man was failing fast. Every day the stench got stronger.

It seemed that Uncle Simon was dying.

Martha could not say that she was sorry.

Oh, Lord, she prayed. *What have I become?*

～

"Lazarus has spoken to you, I assume . . ." Rachel said quietly.

Martha jumped, startled out of her own reverie. She stood in the kitchen area of their home—her place of refuge. It was not large, but it was arranged perfectly to her liking. Even her young sister-in-law had not altered it. Large clay pots of flour and dried beans lined the walls of the room just off the courtyard. Clusters of herbs hung from the ceiling, and dishes sat stacked neatly on low shelves. A shallow grinding basin was built into the courtyard floor opposite the stone oven. Next to it was the largest clay jar of all—the water jar. She pulled her attention to the young woman in front of her.

"Yes," she said, shaking her head at her own unsteadiness. "He spoke to me."

"Well?"

Rachel was younger than Martha by eight years. Eighteen and from a good family, she was pretty, with full lips and large almond eyes. Although she had less life experience than a baby goat, she was the wife and therefore the mistress of the house. She had no mother-in-law to rule her. Martha was only a sister-in-law, who could get her way only by the force of her personality and nothing more. Frankly, it was too exhausting for Martha even to bother.

"You mean, what was the outcome?" Martha asked calmly.

Rachel threw her hands in the air. "Of course! I'm not asking about the weather! What happened?"

"It seems favorable."

"So the arrangements will go forward?"

"They will go forward."

After letting out a squeal, Rachel pulled her veil around her face while she vented a series of happy yelps before she popped her smiling face back out into the open and regarded Martha with expectation. Her expression began to fade, as she received no response from her husband's sister.

"No happiness at all?" the younger woman asked, shaking her head. "Sometimes I believe you have died inside, Martha."

"Will marriage bring happiness?"

"Yes!"

It was such a prompt reply that Martha nearly laughed. Did all marriages bring happiness? Did Aunt Yardena, wife of Simon, achieve happiness through her marriage? Yes, she had gained public honor and respect. And children. But did such things equal happiness? To a girl of Rachel's simple temperament, the answer was easy. As for Martha, the answer was more difficult. The one definite good thing that would come from this marriage was that Martha would no longer be a burden to her brother. She would instead become one to the first wife.

"We'll see," she said after a moment.

Rachel rolled her eyes and shook her head.

"You'll never be happy, Martha," she said in irritation. "Not because the world is so unfair, but because you refuse to be happy!"

"The world is a much more complicated place than you realize."

"But this village is not!"

"What if your husband took a second wife?"

"Then I would rule her!" Rachel laughed.

"If you could have no children?"

Rachel did not answer as the color drained from her face and she gave Martha a peevish look. "No need to be rude," she said finally, turning and walking away.

Martha sighed. The girl was still just a newly married woman. Rachel was not only growing accustomed to being a wife, but she was also adjusting to Lazarus' family, her in-laws. So far she had not conceived. It had been several months, and Rachel showed no signs of being with child. Such a situation was bound to make any new wife nervous. She had only been chosen, not proven herself worthy of the choosing. A child cemented everything.

It had been slightly cruel to bring up such a subject, but Martha had felt forced against the wall. She hated this side of herself—the desperate need to vent her bitterness on everyone. Fiercely resenting naive happiness, it lashed out whenever Martha felt the most afraid.

And this marriage terrified her.

She realized it only now as she stood in the cooler recesses of the house, her veil around her shoulders and her hair uncovered. Moving to the door to the kitchen storage room, her arms crossed over her stomach, she stared into the main room. Two of the four walls were smooth and seemed to glow in their golden hue. The paint had been expensive, and now had begun to chip off the plaster, leaving empty white shapes on the walls that one learned to ignore. They could not afford to have the room repainted. Some luxuries could not be repeated. A straw broom leaned in one corner. Martha could smell the tang of the little goat that lived outside the house, and she inhaled the familiar scent of dung and hay. A scent that normally soothed her, today it set her on edge. Everything in the house seemed to be uncertain, dangerous, and frightening.

It wasn't this house she feared. Nor was it the village, or even the man who wanted to claim her as his own. It was change. Her life with her brother was relatively happy and comfortable. As for the disappointments of her existence, they had become a familiar load that she carried easily enough now, like the way she carried the household water jug on the top of her head. To tip that load, to change the balance . . . could she catch it in time, or would it crash down around her?

Pulling her veil up over her head, she tucked it carefully around her face to hide her hair. Hair was a woman's beauty, and it wasn't for just any man to enjoy. Soon it would be time to send the servant girl to the well for water as well as start preparing the evening meal. Martha and Rachel would bend over the work together. But there were a few minutes still . . .

Rachel gave her an uncertain look as she passed, and Martha returned it with an apologetic smile. She would apologize properly later. After all, she didn't dislike Rachel. The sister-in-law was a good woman and a sweet wife for her brother. Come to think of it, she didn't resent the marriage at all. What she despised lay in her own past.

Martha stepped outside the house. Moments alone were stolen and brief. What did anyone need with time alone when they had a family? A family was an identity, a support. It was both the future and the past. Your family remembered your history and how you fit into the bigger picture, giving you someplace to belong. With a family, why would one ever want to be alone?

But Martha did. Just for a moment, before she returned to the work and the people who needed her. And they did need her—her pragmatism and cooking. They needed her to be Martha, sister of Lazarus.

As she stood at the door to her house, with the dark coolness of the indoors at her back, she looked out over the village. A few women had begun their trek for water from the well. The others would follow shortly. One boy was noisily chasing a fugitive goat that seemed to have eaten something he valued. Some women called their younger children into the house, and an old woman chatted noisily with her neighbor, her throaty voice carrying across the air as she discussed food prices and how irritatingly quickly they were again rising. It was the fault of the Romans, she apparently believed. *She should be silenced, talking like that,* Martha thought quickly. The Romans did not take well to being slandered.

Lord, I always ask You what will become of me. Am I making a mistake in agreeing to the arrangement of this marriage? How can I know? But it is a chance at honor. It is a chance for marriage and children. It is a chance . . .

Her gaze slid from the village life toward the road. It led out of Bethany and toward other larger towns . . . cities of importance. Like Jerusalem—the center of their cultural and religious life. Bethany was not an important destination. Even Jesus had come here only to get away from the crowds and visit with His friend Lazarus.

What will become of me? Who will love me? Will I be alone forever?

Someone was walking up the road, and Martha shaded her eyes. Many people traveled the road, and she nearly turned away in disinterest, but something about the way the woman walked seemed familiar.

Martha squinted against the lowering sun to get a better look. Yes, it was her walk, her silhouette. A sister would know.

Suddenly she felt the sudden urge to cry.

CHAPTER 2

"And when she finds it, she calls her friends and neighbors together and says, 'Rejoice with me; I have found my lost coin.'"

LUKE 15:9

"It's *her?*"

Rachel stood at the doorway of her home, shading her eyes as she looked out. Her stomach seemed to drop within her body, and she swallowed several times, willing the heaving inside her to subside.

"Lazarus!" she called weakly. "Lazarus!"

"I'm here," he said quietly. He had been standing behind her. Martha stood awkwardly facing her sister. Although never regarded as a beauty, Martha still surprisingly resembled the sister who had always been known for her good looks. If it were possible for the plain and the beautiful to look alike, these two sisters did. Yes, it was hard to identify how, but their expressions were alike as well as their features. Only on one face, the features did not create the same effect.

Mary appeared tired. She was saying something to Martha that they could not hear, and the older sister nodded, still keeping a physical distance with her hands at her sides. It was a tense homecoming, to be sure.

"What is she doing here?" Rachel whispered, glancing back at her husband in alarm.

"She is my sister, Rachel, and is under my protection. She is always welcome."

"But she will bring dishonor!" Rachel could feel her voice rising in pitch, and she struggled to control it. "Lazarus, she is your sister, but you know the kind of woman she is."

"Was."

"There is no past tense in the eyes of the village," his wife said quietly. It was not her place to confront her husband. He had made a decision, and she could not cross him. In fact, she had already gone too far, and she clamped her mouth shut.

"It will be all right," he said, stroking one hand down her back. With a sigh, she leaned into his touch. How could one man make her feel so frustrated, yet so weak in the knees at once? Looking back into his dark eyes, she gave him a smile.

"Mary!" Lazarus called, then slipped past Rachel, holding his arms out to his sister. As Mary turned, a smile spread over her face, lighting up her features in a rare display of beauty, even for her.

"My brother!" she exclaimed, and they wrapped their arms around each other, kissing each other's cheeks, first one side, then the other, again and again.

"It is good to see you, Mary," Lazarus said with emotion in his voice. "It has been too long that you've been away."

"I've missed you, too," she replied with feeling. Then she peered past her brother to give a tentative smile at Rachel.

"God be with you, Mary," Rachel said, coming forward. She awkwardly took her sister-in-law's fingers in her own and pecked at her cheeks. The women moved away from each other quickly after the formal greeting, and Rachel looked uncomfortably down at the stony ground. It was at times like these that she wished a veil covering her face was called for. Men might show their emotions openly, but women did not. They were reserved and quiet. Their veils covered more than men would ever know.

"Come inside then," Martha said in a low voice. "We need not make a show for all our neighbors to see."

The neighbors had not come out to welcome Mary. Ordinarily a returning relative would be welcomed by everyone within sight. Friends and neighbors would join the family to prepare a feast in short order, and the entire village would celebrate the occasion. But that was not the case now, and Rachel felt the humiliation of the collective snub. The village was not joining them in this time of welcome. It pretended that Mary did not exist. Their reaction hurt Rachel even more because she was such a new wife and needed the community's approval. She longed for them to assure her that she was doing well in her new role. How did anyone know that they were succeeding if the village did not demonstrate its approval?

Rachel glanced at Martha, scanning her rigid face for something comforting. The older woman was as much of a mother-in-law as she had. Martha was something stable, even when she was being the most obstinate, a woman with some experience even if that did not involve marriage and childbirth. Because Martha had endured much on her own, Rachel had always looked to her for strength and approval.

It was hard for a young woman to get married. Yes, it was a time of celebration, of course, but she always approached it with mixed feelings. While she would be honorable and would begin her role as mother and wife, at the same time she was also leaving the protective home of her father. She would be leaving her mother's side, the one companion she would have had from birth, who talked to her about all her confusions and insecurities. Her mother encouraged her before she left her father's house, and ever after. Now Rachel was expected to function as wife of Lazarus. But there was no mother-in-law to take the place of her own mother. No one to show her the ways of the new home. No one to encourage her and tell her when she was doing well. Except for Martha . . .

As the family went inside, Rachel felt the frigidity of the community on her back like an ominous desert night wind. If she could have prevented Mary's visit, she would have. If only to save them the humiliation from the village!

"What has happened in our little town since I've left those months ago?" Mary asked, her voice betraying some discomfort.

"Crippled Karlan has been working with Timon in his vineyards. The old man died, and he left poor Karlan with a vineyard of his own to work," Martha announced.

"Not really Crippled Karlan anymore."

"No. Not since he was healed. It's strange how even a healed cripple stays a cripple in public opinion, isn't it?"

Rachel noticed a slightly pained look cross over Mary's face. It was the same for her, Rachel thought. Even a reformed prostitute was always a whore in the public eye. In the family eye, too.

"Mary, you must tell us everything!" Lazarus said once they were all settled in the coolness of the house.

After pouring water in a bowl, a cloth wrapped around her waist for drying and her small hands splashing and rubbing with the skill of long practice, the servant girl washed Mary's feet. Rachel felt the pride of having such an experienced girl in their house. She would never embarrass them. The only embarrassment would come from her husband's sister.

Rachel and Martha poured water from pitchers into earthen cups, and took the woven grass covers off of some plates of parched grain and dried dates, offering them first to Lazarus, and then to Mary. Tonight, on her homecoming, Mary would be served as a guest, but tomorrow would be different. She would be expected to act as a woman in that house again and share the workload.

"Aunt Anna sends her love, of course," Mary said. "The family is doing well in Capernaum. Our cousin Shena has already had four children!"

"Four!" Rachel exclaimed, setting down a dish of stewed lentils with a clatter.

"Twins twice," Mary replied, shaking her head. "Soon it will be you, Rachel!"

The young wife couldn't help feeling herself soften toward her wayward sister-in-law. Any words of encouragement seemed to have that impression on her. Was she reverting back to childhood? Where was the strength of womanhood?

"And you?" Rachel asked. "Did our uncle know anyone . . ."

She left the question hanging, resenting herself for even starting it. Had their uncle found her a husband was what she wanted to know. But she knew the answer, even before she saw Mary's awkward shifting.

"My reputation precedes me," Mary said, raising her eyes to give her sister-in-law a level look. "I'm afraid that a man would have to be crazy to wish to take me to his house." Taking a date from a dish, she chewed it slowly, her lips pursing as her tongue did the work.

Rachel felt the heat rising in her face, and she opened her mouth to object, but closed it again. She knew that Mary spoke the truth. Her sister-in-law's hope for an honorable marriage had been the object of her lengthy visit to Aunt Anna. But the success of such a venture had always been doubted. Mary had always been a . . . woman with physical charms. Watching her sensuously eat a date was embarrassing. Rachel had the urge to pull her veil across her own face. It was possible to love Mary and hate her all in the same moment.

"There is only one Man with a heart big enough to forgive the likes of me," Mary said softly, looking back down to her lap. "How can I expect the same treatment from a mere human being?"

She spit the date pit onto her plate.

"Martha has a wedding being arranged," Rachel said, more to change the subject than to offer information.

When Martha pinched Rachel's leg through her robes, Rachel darted her husband's sister a quick, apologetic look. Unfortunately, Martha's privacy had to be sacrificed to ease the awkward moment.

"Really?" Mary said, her face breaking into a smile. "How soon? And to whom?"

"The details are still being worked out," Lazarus said. "But the man is Jebuseh."

Something passed over Mary's face as quick as the fluttering of a moth, then disappeared.

"You'll be very happy, Martha," she said. "I hope you won't forget me in your new good fortune!"

They could not ask what had flashed through Mary's mind at the mention of Jebuseh's name. Of course, Rachel had her own suspicions that it involved Mary's old profession. Martha, if she had eyes at all in her head, would assume the same. But that could not be spoken of.

"I hope to be," Martha said simply. "You should know that there is another wife. I would be the second."

"But it is a chance to have children," Mary said matter of factly. "And children are a blessing, are they not?"

"Yes," her sister acknowledged, her lips tightening.

"You will be happy."

"Thank you."

Martha's reply was a little clipped, and Rachel glanced toward her curiously. The woman's eyes were reserved and calm, but her heart, Rachel knew, would be in a much different state.

"Uncle Simon is ill," Martha announced.

For the first time, Mary and Martha exchanged a look that seemed to speak much between them. What it meant Rachel could not guess, but she could sense the enormity of understanding that had just passed between the two sisters, their eyes locked.

"How ill?" Mary asked.

"He will likely die."

"Don't say that!" Rachel interrupted. "It is bad luck. You don't want him to die! He is family, after all!"

"I did not say I wanted him to die," Martha said, turning her flat gaze onto Rachel for the first time. "I simply said he will likely die."

"How soon?" Mary asked.

"Only God knows," Martha replied.

Mary seemed to age before them. The lines around her mouth became more pronounced, and her eyes darkened into bottomless wells.

"He will not die soon," Lazarus insisted. "The old man has seen worse illnesses than this! We won't lose him yet. He's been like a father to us. I can see how this bad news affects you, Mary. But don't let your heart break for him yet. He will pull through!"

"He's been especially kind to me," Rachel added.

He had been. Uncle Simon had given her some beautiful clothes for a wedding present, and he had told her how lovely she was, and how happy he was to have such a girl as her join their family. Hugging her and patting her shoulder, he had told her that she would have many children. Uncle Simon had been kind to her, and something inside of her had melted. Again, what had happened to the strength of womanhood?

Mary looked at Martha questioningly.

"He has been kind to her," her sister affirmed.

Why she would not be believed, Rachel did not know. She did not like this. The two sisters frightened her. They were distant and cold with each other, but even over the distance, they seemed to share more information that Rachel could comprehend. Martha, always the resolute, firm one, seemed to have changed. Rachel did not like the transformation. It was not the Martha that she had grown to love! This was another woman, with too many secrets. Mary was to blame.

"Uncle Simon said he hoped I had daughters," Rachel continued.

"I hope you have sons," Martha said quietly.

"He wanted me to have daughters so that his grandsons would have quality wives."

"I hope you have boys that are strong and defiant," Mary said slowly, her eyes gradually meeting Rachel's. "I hope you have boys who fight and band together, and protect you."

What was this? Rachel frowned, looking from one sister to the other. This was strange. Since when did the two ever agree?

"Like their father, of course," Martha said with a wink, immediately dispelling the tense moment.

Laughing, Rachel looked shyly up at her husband.

"There will be quality girls enough, my wife," Lazarus said with a good-humored laugh of his own. "Give me sons!"

Of course, a man wanted sons. What one didn't? Except for Uncle Simon. Rachel thought he must be a gentle man to like daughters so much. He must have a soft heart, a mind that could understand women. She liked him for that. And she liked him for hoping that she had daughters.

"One of your uncle's servants wants to see you," the servant girl murmured, bending down next to Lazarus. He glanced uneasily toward his wife, then nodded.

"I will be there momentarily." He rose to his feet with a small grunt. The veins in his hands had stood out as he pushed himself upward. Lazarus was a handsome man, this husband of hers. Rachel watched him leave the room, her eyes following him, even when the door closed after him.

"Help in the kitchen, would you?" Martha said, glancing toward her sister.

"As if I wouldn't?" Mary asked, her peaceful exterior seeming to crack like a clay bowl under too much pressure.

"It hasn't been your strength, that's all," Martha said with a cool smile.

"I am a woman in this house, am I not?"

"It was only a reminder."

Rachel couldn't help smiling to herself. Mary and Martha would be elderly, bent over walking sticks, and they would still be nattering at each other! They each stooped and picked up a serving dish, then walked serenely toward the kitchen area, heads held high at the exact same angle. They disappeared into the courtyard kitchen just as Lazarus returned.

"Is there news?" Rachel asked, suddenly feeling anxious as she saw her husband's somber expression.

"Yes."

She silently waited for him to elaborate.

"Uncle Simon is much worse."

Lazarus looked down into his wife's eyes, putting his hands gently on her shoulders. His dark beard fell down to well below his collarbone, and she reached up to stroke the wiry curls with one hand.

"I know you love our uncle," Lazarus said quietly. "I'm sorry, Rachel, but it looks bad."

"How bad?" she whispered, feeling her throat constrict.

"We should go there tonight. The family will need our support in a time like this."

Rachel knew what this meant. It was Martha's fault. She had mentioned it—said the words and tempted fate. Everyone knew it was bad luck to speak of death, and Martha had brought it down on them as swiftly as a swung ax! Poor Martha—she hadn't been thinking properly. Her sister had bewitched her. Rachel couldn't blame Martha. But as for Mary . . . Ill omens, it seemed, followed that woman straight into their home!

CHAPTER 3

"By their fruit you will recognize them. Do people pick grapes from thornbushes, or figs from thistles?"

MATTHEW 7:16

Martha crept forward, letting her rust-colored woolen veil fall back down to her shoulders. She wasn't used to wearing such heavy fabric over her head. It felt awkward, and it kept sliding off, slipping down her hair like water off a dove's back. Her mother refused to let her tie it. A woman of quality did not secure her veil by tying it. Instead, she knew how to move so that she remained fully swathed in the draped material. It was a skill she must learn. Martha glanced back at Mary, still too young to receive a veil yet. Although only a year younger, she looked like such a child! Martha, a full 8 years old, felt the responsibility of her years keenly.

Mary giggled behind her, and Martha turned around to dart her a severe look. The younger sister clamped her hand over her mouth, her eyes widening in glee and excitement. They weren't supposed to be out of their beds. It was well past their bedtime, and the adult conversation was not for their young ears. Because they knew this, it was precisely why they had come, sneaking barefoot from their beds.

"We'd better not get caught!" Martha whispered.

"We won't! Just be quiet!"

Squeezing her mouth shut once more, Mary watched her older sister with wide eyes. Her little sister looked like a mouse, Martha thought, her eyes so big, and her hair a dusty brown color. Such an awkward child. Martha wondered if the girl would ever be pretty. Her arms and legs were as thin as twigs, her eyes were way too large in her head, and she had a smile that was so wide it was almost shocking.

Their father's house was quite large, with several rooms used for sleeping and living. In the central courtyard, where the cooking fire was, the adults would sit together and talk late into the night with the smells of that evening's supper still lingering in the air. Uncle Simon would come to visit sometimes, and they could hear his booming laugh through the walls. The house seemed enormous to Martha, however. She felt like a spy, sneaking through a palace.

Uncle Simon was not her father's favorite sibling, but Moseh had only one brother.

"I have only one," he had always said. Martha had sensed that her father meant something more by this, but she didn't understand. Her parents had always discouraged contact between her and her uncle. Nothing was said directly, but there were looks and subtle hints in body language that let Martha know that her uncle was not someone to feel friendly with. *He must not like children,* she decided early. *Perhaps he must find them tiresome or they must make him angry.*

"Shhh!" Martha warned as they crept closer to the door. They could hear the voices, rumbling and murmuring over adult secrets. The men were talking. Women did not participate in male conversation. Their mother would be making herself busy with serving the two men, her ears open and eager. How else would a woman know what was happening in the men's sphere? How else would she be able to anticipate her husband's needs?

"The field costs too much," her father was saying. "It isn't worth it. The soil is rocky and not easy to plow."

"It will be worth more when Roshan's son finally marries. Perhaps he will marry up, get a good dowry, and buy it back from you at a profit," Uncle Simon suggested.

"It seems wrong to exploit a young man newly married," their father said.

"Not married yet," Uncle Simon laughed. "Slow to start!"

"I will think about it."

"Think quickly. I might buy it first, brother!"

"Then do so. I won't stop you."

"I try to help you get ahead," Simon said, his voice turning dark. "You refuse the help. You are my responsibility, and you insist on sullying my name with your poverty."

"We are not poor." Their father's voice had gained an edge as well. "We are honest."

"God gives opportunities as well as wealth."

"God's blessing may be on the wealthy. But it cannot remain while they defy God's laws."

"What is this?" Simon's voice turned cajoling. "We are brothers! We are family! Let us act like it! Let us act together for the bettering of our children!"

"I agree. But let us not take advantage of our neighbor."

"Why should we not take what we can?" Simon sounded exasperated. "If we do not take it, it will evaporate and be gone!"

"Then take what you can! A narrow, rocky field is not worth the moral questioning. But let us stop this arguing before we fight outright!"

Mary edged closer to Martha. They were discussing the sale of a field, that much was obvious. But the girls didn't understand it. It was men's worries, not women's. Was this what they talked about when the children were in bed? Fields and money? Mary looked bored, and her mouth opened in a wide yawn, her mouth so much larger than any other child's. It was not the excitement they had expected. Martha had hoped for secrets of fortune, stories of deceit and the hard bargaining for marriages. Instead, the men argued about the sale of a field.

Yet it was a learning experience—one about men. So emotional, men were. Always ready to fight and shout over something. Women were different. If they did not agree, they would become silent, and often ignore each other while their feelings continued to rage within. It was not a woman's place to display her emotions on her sleeve. Mary and Martha already fully understood this. Men, however, were different creatures entirely, and the girls were always a little surprised at what emerged from them.

"It's that dog again!" their father suddenly said, turning his attention to the outside door. "Our goat's milk will be soured yet!"

Standing, he made his way briskly to the door, picking up a stick on the way. The dog would be sorry if he caught it, the girls knew. Something inside of Martha felt sad about the beating it would receive, but their father had to protect the goat. It gave them milk, while dogs were wild beasts, scavenging in the streets.

"I'll get my cloak, brother!" Simon called out the open front door. "Until tomorrow, then!"

Their uncle continued to stare out after his brother.

"Think about it!" he added, his voice raised. "Roshan is willing to sell that field now, but for how long?"

He didn't get a reply, as their father was preoccupied with a growling, snapping mutt. The animal had been getting too bold lately. They'd had trouble with it before. Martha thought that it must be hungry. Her mother had told her that hungry dogs ate small goats, and sometimes small girls. The girl tried not to feel hurt for the dog while it yelped.

Suddenly she held her breath. Her mother had left the room. It was not proper for her to be with her husband's brother alone. Part of the girl knew it was time to retreat, but she could not pull herself away.

Turning, Uncle Simon walked toward their hiding spot with a measured pace. He came closer and closer, and Martha's breath caught in her throat. She could feel her sister quivering next to her. Both knew the punishment—they would be beaten! They would be beaten worse for the embarrassment of being seen misbehaving in front of their uncle!

Martha's heart pounded in her small chest, and she pushed herself backward, trying to shove Mary away from her and back to their sleeping quarters.

"What is this? Girls out of bed?"

Uncle Simon looked down at them, disgust glinting in his eyes.

Opening her mouth to speak, Martha couldn't make a squeak. She closed it again. Nothing she said could help her now.

"Your father should beat you!" he said in a low voice. "If I told him . . ."

He let the threat hang in the air. Martha could feel his strong breath brushing against her face. He crouched down, staring her in the eye. Slowly he licked his lips, flicking his gaze behind Martha toward Mary.

"Uncle Simon won't tell," he said after a moment, a slow smile gradually crossing his face.

Martha reached back, clutching her sister's sweaty fingers. "We're sorry, sir," she breathed. "We are wicked, and very sorry!"

"You are wicked. And wicked children need to be in bed."

But when Martha lurched forward, Mary did not come with her.

"Come on!" the older girl hissed, looking back, but her sister sat with eyes wide and terrified, Uncle Simon's hand solidly on her shoulder.

"Go to bed, Martha," he said. "Mary will be along in a few minutes. Uncle Simon will talk to her."

Turning, Martha dashed toward their bedroom, her stomach filled with dread. She couldn't go back and follow Mary now. If she were caught, they both would be beaten. It was best to obey—to be a good girl and do as told.

So Martha lay down in her bed, her eyes wide open, her hands trembling. She waited and waited. Finally little Mary came back to bed. She crawled under the cover, curled into a small ball, and lay in silence.

"Mary!" Martha whispered.

Her sister didn't answer.

"Mary!"

"I'm sleeping now."

And so Martha tried to sleep. But all she could dream of was a large switch that wanted to beat them, and Uncle Simon standing by with his strange smile.

Simon pushed himself up onto his elbow, grunting with the effort. Where was that no-good woman? She was forever crouching over him, suffocating him, when he wanted rest. But when he needed something, she was nowhere to be found.

His mouth was parched, his lips pasty, and he could feel the sticky film at the corners of his mouth. He knew that he must smell like sickness, but he could not sense the odor himself. By now he was used to it. All he smelled was musty air.

"Woman!" he croaked.

No reply.

"Yardena! Woman!"

Nothing.

Reaching for his bowl of water, he pulled it closer, spilling half the contents on the ground. He muttered to himself in misery. His body ached, his eyes were on fire, and he was covered in a thick sweat. After raising the bowl to his quivering lips he slurped up the remaining water. The clay bowl slipped from his fingers and clattered hollowly to the floor beside him.

Exhausted, he fell back against his sleeping mat, shut his eyes, and breathed deeply. How could this have happened?

He was a robust man. He was strong! He was virile! So how did this sickness overcome him so easily? Only a month ago he was celebrating at the wedding of one of his neighbor's sons—dancing, eating, drinking . . . When his wife whispered that maybe he had drunk enough for one evening, he had begun shouting at her to go home.

Now he couldn't even speak loud enough to make her come to him and bring him some decent water. Here he was flat on his back, and she had lost all respect. If he only felt better, he'd make her regret that!

Now, his nephew's wife—she was the one he wanted near him. His wife tired him. But Rachel was beautiful and young. She looked at him with appropriate fear and melted at a kind word. The woman jumped when he spoke. Rachel was pretty, and she knew how to respect someone above her. He had chosen well for Lazarus—had done well by the boy. Sure, Lazarus had pointed her out to him, but Simon had approved and made the marriage happen. Lazarus would always speak well of him for this, even long after Simon was dead and entombed.

Dead. He didn't want to think of it. After all, he was not an old man. It was too soon to die. There was too much he still had to do. If he took another wife he could sire more children. And he could have more dinners, throw more parties . . .

But he had faced the fear of his own mortality before. There had been another time in his life he'd looked death in the face. It was two years earlier, and he had truly believed that he would die, alone and ignored.

Feared and loathed, leprosy was a disgusting disease. He hadn't realized that he had the condition at first, since it had appeared on skin normally covered by his clothing. But then he noticed the white flakes of dead skin. As the disease persisted and seemed to spread, he became terrified. Although he hid the condition for a long time, it eventually grew more visible. Someone noticed it, and word spread.

Under the flaking patches of skin there was exposed flesh. When he scratched, he bled, and when he bled, infection set in. And the more he tried to hide it, the faster it spread. Crusty infection mingled with the dead skin.

One day the priests came. Careful not to touch anything in his home, they examined him, conversed softly together, and declared him "unclean." The village elders immediately sent him to a nearby leper colony.

The place was horrible, indescribable. The desperate people fought each other over the food baskets that their families would bring and leave outside the camp for them. Men would steal from children.

Home was so close, yet so far. He could walk there in an hour or less, but he could never return. No longer could he hold his wife or seduce his mistress. Never again could he play with his children or relax at a feast. It was over. Simon had become one more of the walking dead.

God was punishing him. He knew it. The Lord was wreaking vengeance on him for the things he had done. For people he had cheated, promises he had not kept. Simon had lost God's favor, after years of righteous living as a Pharisee. Because God had turned His face away, Simon's flesh was falling away in showers of dry flakes.

But then another leper heard of Jesus. How He healed people and touched lepers. Everyone knew that leprosy passed from person to person by touch, but this healer did not fear to touch their disease-ridden bodies with His hands! And they were made well. Or so the stories went.

What did he have to lose? He went with nine other men who were equally desperate. They would all die soon. Weak from infection, they'd been vomiting even the stolen bits of food they managed to scavenge. If they could summon the strength to make the journey to search out this man, what did they have to lose?

Finding the crowds was easy. Parting them was easier still. People ran and gave little screams, trying to get out of the way. And when they saw Jesus, He was not quite what Simon had expected. Although He was tall and strong, He looked more like the carpenter He had been than a miraculous healer. Quietly He simply reached out and touched each one of them, saying it was their faith that made them well again. He looked into Simon's eyes, and Simon felt as if the man was reading his very soul. It was eerie, and he didn't like it. And when he looked down to break the eye contact, he saw that his flesh was whole again. His skin was smooth and unblemished, and the only stinking smell that remained came from the bandages that he quickly tore from his body in disgust.

"Go to the priests!" Jesus said. "Be declared well."

And so they stumbled over each other, rushing to be the first to be declared well . . . rushing to be the first to return to their previous lives. Simon noticed one turn back, and he felt a plunge of relief that he had one less competitor in the race to the Temple.

What had that man gone back for? He couldn't fathom. Who would be stupid enough to pause, or let another get ahead of him? Had he gone back to ask for another miracle? Perhaps for a family member?

Simon wondered if he had been stupid not to go back and ask for another miracle. But he did not want to offend the healer; he didn't want his healing reversed. No, he decided, the one who had gone back was stupid. But what was that to him? It was necessary to have foolish people in the world so that one could pass them in the race.

The priests declared him healed. He did not make it first to the Temple, but he ran hard, and at the age of 50, that was a feat in itself. The exhilaration of being told he was now clean and able to return to his family was enough to stop his heart in his chest.

Returning home, he pushed through the familiar front door, and looked down at his wife, who was grinding flour on a saddle quern in the courtyard.

"Wife, give me food."

Yardena's face went from shock to confusion to happiness, and she rushed about putting together a meal for him. All the while she spilled out questions.

"What happened? How are you back? Are you well again? How did it happen?"

That was his wife. She was his again. He was man of this house once more. His life was his again!

"Wife, come here!" he barked, and she skidded to a stop, her eyes wide in alarm. She moved carefully toward him, then ducked her head in submission.

Putting his arms around her, he held her close. In the leper colony he'd dreamed of feeling his wife against him. She was stiff in his arms at first, alarmed at this strange show of affection. Normally he saved all contact for the night. But he held her tightly, ignoring her discomfort until she began to relax into his embrace, and her tears started to soak into his tunic.

And now he lay on his bed, and the wife who had been so moved by his return only two years ago was nowhere to be found. Here he was dying, and she was out working in the front of the house with the goat, or possibly gone to the market, or out visiting a friend.

What kind of woman listened to her husband when he told her to get out of his sight? She should have known better and crouched within earshot until she heard him call for her.

Rachel would not do that. No, he'd chosen well for Lazarus. His nephew's wife would have crept back into the room and bathed his head with cool water. That's what Rachel would have done . . .

Simon's eyes closed once more. He could see red spots through his eyelids, and he moaned in discomfort.

I am not old, he thought to himself. *Why is this happening to me?*

And then he drifted off into a fitful sleep in which he dreamed of a dog that kept growling at him, sounding so close, but he could never see the mongrel so that he could kick it.

CHAPTER 4

"But I tell you that anyone who looks at a woman lustfully has already committed adultery in his heart."

MATTHEW 5:28

Yardena put the last of the flat barley loaves onto the platter and stopped to look at it. The floury brown disks were in a jumbled heap. She adjusted the bread again. It would have to do. Ordinarily the circles of bread would have been more uniform in size, but her mind wasn't on her work today.

The family was here, and she had a roomful of men to serve. Her daughters had come with their husbands, and her sons were as hungry as always. Lazarus had also stopped by—bringing *both* sisters with him. It was disappointing that Mary had to come home at a time like this. She had looked out her door and seen the woman approaching her home, but Yardena had purposefully ignored her. It was bad enough that Mary was a relative!

Yardena felt a surge of pride as she glanced around her cooking area. It was a good home, constructed of plastered stone rubble with solid wooden support beams. The second level had sleeping mats, and a place to sit outside on the roof under a canopy of multi-colored fabric. The fabric itself announced their status in the village. Her house was larger than other people's. She had enough food available to serve many guests. The village respected her. Her husband had been a wealthy man.

Had been? Why did she think that? He was not dead yet. And he was still a wealthy man. When he did die, he would do it honorably.

She had put him to rest in her own mind when he had gotten leprosy. The condition was dishonorable. It made her distasteful in the public eye. People avoided her, as if her husband's disease might have rubbed off on her clothing. And it might have, for all she knew! But when he came back, they forgot—if you could say that a village ever forgets. But they did, at least, respect his wealth and his position. The priests had declared him well—who were they to counter the priestly verdict?

When Yardena had married Simon, she had only been 15. Her parents had arranged the match, and she had only had sense to thank them some five years after her marriage. They had chosen well. Simon was moody, yes. He was irritable and demanding. But he was also very wealthy and influential. What did it matter if he were gentle and sweet indoors or a snorting ox? The only thing that mattered was what people saw. And they observed power. Power that she had married.

That was not saying that life with Simon had been easy. No, it was not. She had to work twice as hard as other wives, she was sure. Not in the housework, but in the other areas of life that demanded a woman's touch. Like smoothing over irritations when Simon's temper got the better of him, and skillfully steering the young Martha in another direction when her uncle had slipped into one of his dark moods. But it had paid off! The other women were careful around her. They were grateful to be invited to her home for a dinner and looked up to her. When they gossiped they were wary. Birds of the air might report their words, after all, and that would not be good for anyone. Yardena was a success in life!

"Aunt Yardena, what can I do to help?"

She looked at her niece with an indulgent smile. Martha had

always been a good girl. So helpful and decent. It was too bad that she hadn't been blessed with the kind of face that attracted a man's attention, but she had still grown into a sweet woman.

"Take this platter in to the men, would you?"

With a smile Martha hoisted the heavy polished metal platter to her shoulder. That platter was another symbol of the position Yardena and her husband held in the community. Lazarus could not afford such a luxury. It was why Yardena was showing it off today.

Her daughters were kneading dough, their attention focused on the task at hand. They were good wives, her girls. They knew how to work hard, and they had the looks to keep their husbands interested. She glanced proudly at their straight backs and shining black hair. The younger, Shiloh, was a little too plump. And the older, Tisha, had a nose that was a little too pronounced. But on the whole, they were admirable. And they listened to their mother when she advised them on how to deal with their in-laws.

Yes, Yardena had honor. She had done well. Two girls and two boys had survived of all her children. It was accepted that babies died. When they did, a mother simply never spoke of them. Perhaps the death had been a punishment. Or maybe it had simply been God's will. Whatever the reason, a woman did not need to advertise personal pain. One simply never spoke of it again.

And now, when her husband died, which she feared he would . . . now he would leave them honorably, and she could mourn. But she would mourn for more than her husband. Yardena would mourn for the babies that had died. She would mourn the misery her husband had put her through. And she would mourn for her new needy situation, being without a husband to protect her. Life would not be the same without Simon. Part of her wondered if it wouldn't be a little easier. Another part would miss his sporadic tenderness. And still another part of her would even miss his bellowing voice. Through the years she had gotten accustomed to him. In fact, she might even say she had become fond of him—when he was in his good moods.

A lump rose in her throat. Yes, she would miss him more than she admitted. Twenty years spent with a man could not be forgotten so easily. Eight children born were a testament to something, were they not? Maybe he would not die. God willing, he would pull through this time! Maybe the doctors were all wrong, and Simon would *prove* it when, standing before them strong and robust, he called them down publicly for their stupidity.

Yes, that was it. He was simply ill, that was all. He had been ill before. Who hadn't been? No need to think of the other . . . *Don't bother with it!* she ordered herself.

"Mother, you are crying into the lentils," Shiloh said. "Wipe your eyes with your veil. It will be all right, Mother . . ."

Yardena shook her head and dabbed at her eyes. "I'm not crying—it's the onions."

"You are, and who would blame you?" Tisha asked. "Oh, Mother, this is a hard time for you!"

Their mother put her arms around her two girls, who had come to her side. One tall and slender, causing her to reach up to pull the woman close. The younger daughter was short and stout. She hugged them tightly with all her strength. Her gray-streaked hair mingled with her daughters' black locks, and she let out a shaky sigh.

"God will provide," she said with more assuredness than she felt. "God will provide . . . And when your father is feeling better, he will scold me for serving the guests too slowly!"

Shiloh and Tisha quickly looked at each other.

"Stop exchanging glances," Yardena snapped. "Like I am not even in the room!"

"Oh, and there is Martha, finishing our bread!" Shiloh said, her voice barely concealing her annoyance.

"If it is tough, we'll know why," Tisha murmured.

"Forgive me," Martha said, the color rising in her cheeks. "I only wanted to help."

"It was good of you!" Yardena said, pinching Tisha's bare arm. "I think Martha knows that her uncle is not at death's door, don't you, Martha?"

A pause.

"God only knows, aunt," Martha said finally. "And God's ways are not man's ways."

Yardena took a deep breath, wiped her eyes once more, and turned her attention back to the stewed lentils she was preparing.

"Send the servant for fresh water," she announced. "More people may be arriving, and they will have dusty feet to be washed."

She was back in control.

⌐⌐⌐

Martha placed the flat loaves of bread in the small baked clay oven, heated by coals glowing below it, and wiped the sweat from her forehead. Her sleeves were tied back behind her, leaving her arms bare. Now she stood, stretching her back.

It was an awkward time . . . the days before a death. And she was doing the only thing she knew how: helping with the kitchen work. It was the only way she knew to show her support. Her cousins resented her presence. She wasn't a simpleton, and their attitudes might as well have been woven into their robes, it was so obvious. But what else was there for her to do?

Things would be different, though. Unmarried now, she was not on equal footing with her cousins. They were above her, married women with children of their own. Yes, Martha was unmarried. Unwanted. Unchosen. Underfoot in the kitchen. But soon she would be married, too. She would be one of them—would be equal.

Jebuseh seemed to be a good man. And wealthy. His wife did wear fine clothing. He wasn't known to frequent prostitutes. Her sister's flickered expression at the mention of the man's name worried her . . . But nothing was proven. And what other offers did Martha have?

She would be known as wife of Jebuseh . . . wife of Jebuseh . . . It had a nicer ring to it than daughter of Moseh, or sister of Lazarus. As a wife, she would be legitimate—respected.

Martha could sense a smile twitching at her lips, and she did her best to stifle it. If all went well, not only would she be a wife, but she would be a mother, as well. Children would bring her respect . . . finally after so many years of being pitied.

But that fluttering expression that crossed Mary's face at the mention of Jebuseh's name still nagged at her mind. Could she marry a man who had bedded her own sister?

"Wife! Woman!"

The shout from the bedroom was hoarse and weak. Aunt

Yardena's head popped up from the lentil stew she had been preparing, and her eyes widened in a look of alarm. It was a strange expression to have when one's husband called—in an ordinary home, that is. But it was a typical expression to cross the faces of the women in this house.

"Your father is calling me," she murmured, and Martha looked at her cousins. Their heads had dropped in a sudden interest in the work before them.

Aunt Yardena wiped her hands on a cloth and disappeared into the house. The sleeping chamber was behind the kitchen and furthest from the general living area where the men had gathered to talk. The sexes stayed separate, and since the men had the priority, they had the comfort of pillows and mats. The women, expected to serve, thus spent their time in the cooking area, away from the men. The smoky courtyard was their domain.

It was a large home. Poorer ones did not have the luxury of so many different rooms. Many had only a single room. A cooking fire, that also gave warmth in the cold months, was in the center. Living, sleeping, eating—it all happened there. If the quarters were too cramped, the household moved outside to sit under tarps. Except during the raining season, the outdoors would be the most comfortable.

Uncle Simon, however, was wealthy. He had a sleeping area built onto his roof and a separate cooking area so that the men needn't be bothered by the women's presence. It was a comfortable home in which people liked to congregate.

"Stupid and slow!"

The words were loud enough for the women to hear out in the courtyard, and they exchanged guilty glances. It was shameful to hear such a thing—it was humiliating for everyone.

"Where were you? Didn't you hear me moaning? No respect, that's what it is! You wish me dead. But I won't die yet, woman! Not yet!"

Martha cleared her throat and looked away from her cousins, her face hot with embarrassment. The day was not so warm that the heat baked her. It was cool enough that she didn't feel sticky with sweat being so close to the fire. The rainy season approached, and with it frigid nights.

"Get out! You disgust me! I don't even want it! Get me water, and crawl out of this room like you deserve."

Aunt Yardena returned, her expression grim and her hands shaking as she tried to grip her robes to calm them. Tears filled her eyes, and her lips were pressed together in a thin line.

"He's in pain," she said apologetically to no one in particular. "Such a dear man, but the pain gets to him."

"Mother, I can bring him the water," Tisha said in a low voice. "Stay here. It is all right."

"Whatever for? He needs me. In a time like this, a man needs the wife he was joined to in his youth. Simon wants me with him."

Tisha fell back, watching her mother warily as she dipped water from the water jar, pouring it into a clay cup. She spilled some down her hands and onto her feet, but she pressed on, dipping and pouring, dipping and pouring, and spilling like a child. Her hands continued to shake. The earthen cup did not seem to want to fill.

Martha pulled her veil over her head. It was a relief to feel the fabric against her hair, shielding her face from view. A veil could be a woman's best friend. She murmured a few words of excuse— something about the smoke and needing some fresh air to clear her eyes. None of the women listened. Not that they ever did. It was her role to listen to them, her place to comfort their sorrows. They did not notice her slip out of the house.

Once outside, she took in a deep breath. The village of Bethany was situated on the eastern slope of the Mount of Olives along the Jericho road. Jesus spent a good deal of time there. He liked the solitude and the opportunity to be able to pray away from the crowds that constantly and hopefully followed him. And not far away the Roman authorities crucified criminals. She tried to push the memories away. Crucifixion was hideous, but it was the Romans' favorite punishment. Some days the crosses were as plentiful as stubble in a mown field, and despite the horror of the punishment, people became accustomed to seeing it. Still, she tried to push any thought of it out of her mind.

The low mountain ridge, draped in olive groves, was a golden sight when the sun rose, bathing the eastern slopes in its first rays. Bethany was only a short distance from Jerusalem, but the village was quiet and dull. Martha had always liked its peacefulness. At times, though, that peacefulness seemed more like that noisy void one heard in the ears before falling to the ground in a faint.

The air was fresh, and Martha looked at the sun setting over the top of the mountain ridge. The sky glowed red and orange, and she could feel the cool of the evening settling over her. The line of shadow had already moved up the mountains, and the village lay in the dim pool of night, even though the sun still illuminated the sky in its last crimson light.

The village had one road that led through it . . . one main road that meandered toward Jerusalem. Along it stood the most important houses. Martha stared up the road, and sighed when she saw the all-too-familiar form of her sister. Some things about her sister would never change. Mary stood a little ways down the road, in the company of a man.

Their cousin, actually. Jacob. Elder son of Simon, their uncle. Cocky and self-important, he was married and had six children. His father's death would bring him control of all the old man's wealth. He had acted the part of master since he was a boy. Now he was a grown man in his 30s. His beard was neatly trimmed, and his robes were expensive and flowed in a way that only a heavy purse could buy. Head uncovered, he stood confidently, looking down at his cousin attentively. A handsome man, Martha had to admit.

The noise from the house was subdued, considering the number of people inside. But this was not an ordinary gathering. They were there to bring support in a time of trial . . . were there to grieve once the old man passed. It was not a time for loud laughter and joking.

Mary and Jacob were talking quietly, it seemed. Martha shook her head. In the middle of town, at that! Did her sister never learn? It wouldn't take long for the news of her little walk to reach the ears of Jacob's wife. A well-respected woman, she would soon be mistress of her husband's inheritance. Jacob's wife would not like her husband's name being trampled. She wouldn't want her husband to be with the likes of Mary, whether the conversation was innocent or not. What woman would?

The pair had turned and started back toward Uncle Simon's house. Soon to be Jacob's house. Mary looked down, her expression calm and unassuming. Jacob's attention was fixed on his pretty cousin's down-turned eyes. Now, as they walked back, pieces of their conversations floated on the night breezes back toward Martha. They didn't see her. Few people did, she noted ruefully.

"I had missed you," Jacob was saying. "You were gone a long time."

"It's nice to be missed by my family." She said something else, but Martha didn't catch it.

"It wasn't the same without you," he went on.

Mary did not reply.

"You must be lonely now."

"I am. But that is my punishment, I suppose. For being the woman I was."

"A great many men miss you, cousin," he said with a coarse laugh.

Martha felt the heat rise in her face as Mary suddenly stiffened. Jacob's sympathy, it seemed, had an ulterior motive.

"You were kind to me, I remember," he continued. "But you refused to favor me."

Mary remained silent.

"Come now, you said you were lonely!"

"Will you take me to your home for dinner, then, cousin?" Mary asked coldly, turning her face toward him. "Will you bring me as a guest, along with my brother? Will you allow me to work in the kitchen alongside your wife?"

"Hardly!" he exclaimed. "How could you imagine such a thing?"

"Because that would alleviate much loneliness, cousin," she said icily. "To be accepted as a woman in the community would do much for me, cousin."

"I could keep you comfortable. I'm coming into my father's fortune, you know. I could simply say that I am providing for my family. You are family, Mary, after all. Would I hurt my family?"

"You have hurt your wife already." Mary pulled her veil around her head. "Whether she knows her dishonor or not, you have hurt *her*."

Poor Mary. Martha suddenly had a vision of her sister as small girl again . . . a small girl who knew too much. Would it never end? Would she always be *this*—a prostitute in public opinion? Would she always be *that* woman? Not tonight!

"Good evening, cousin!" Martha called, walking toward them.

The two glanced up quickly. Jacob's eyes darkened in dislike, and Mary had the decency to appear embarrassed.

"It's very late to be out," Martha said, looking around herself. "For me, a spinster, I am not missed, but you, cousin, the direct heir of an ill man! You will be missed!"

"It was hot indoors," he said smoothly. "I saw my cousin and wanted to welcome her home again. My family had missed their obligations there . . ."

"Where is your wife, cousin?" Martha asked pointedly.

"Do you suggest that your sister lured me outside for something unbecoming?" he inquired, his eyes wide and innocent. "You don't think much of your sister!"

"I simply ask where your wife is. She did not join us in the kitchen."

"Martha, Martha," he said with a low laugh. "Always in the kitchen."

"I owe her a visit."

"Our child has a fever," he replied, the laughter evaporating from his voice. "She is at home, doing her duty as mother and wife."

The stab was obvious.

"She is a good woman," Martha said with an even smile. "I will compliment her when I next see her. I will tell her how kind you have been to my sister. So dutiful, you are."

His dark eyes narrowed, and Martha nearly took a step backward at the pure venom she saw in them. He hated her. She'd known it for years. Feelings were always distilled into the strongest potions within a family. Martha was a spinster, representing something that no one much liked.

"If you would be so kind as to wait for an invitation," Jacob said. "Now, my dear cousins, I must go back inside." He eyed them once more before striding away.

An invitation would not be forthcoming. And Martha's threat was palpable. She would not talk, of course. She never did. But she was a woman who knew secrets, whether she wanted to or not. Secrets held power.

"Good evening, sister," Martha said, giving Mary a tight smile.

"Thank you," Mary said in a low voice. "I don't like our cousin much."

"You are needed in the kitchen," Martha said tersely. "As usual."

For a moment Mary looked at her sister, her eyes sad. "I know," she said finally. "I'll go in."

And Mary started toward the kitchen area—like a woman walking deliberately toward a rabid dog or someone about to throw herself onto a fire. She knew the reception waiting for her from the "proper" women. From the wives who hated her.

Martha sighed. Part of her pitied her sister. It deeply saddened her that Mary would never be accepted. Even when Martha became an honorable wife, her sister would be on the outside. Forever looking in and not belonging. And Martha was not stupid enough to let Mary within a stone's throw of her new husband!

But another part of her hated her sister too. Detested her for being that kind of woman, selling her body and bringing shame to the family. It humiliated her that men still saw her sister as the prostitute. She hated her sister's unwittingly alluring manner. So sensuous, even when she was trying to act with decorum. Always moving with such swaying grace, without ever thinking about it. So physical. So ripe. She had a way of acting almost naked, even with her veil pulled up to her eyes. What woman *wouldn't* hate Mary?

"Oh, God!" Martha prayed. "Why must she be *mine?*"

CHAPTER 5

"Do not give dogs what is sacred; do not throw your pearls to pigs. If you do, they may trample them under their feet, and then turn and tear you to pieces."

MATTHEW 7:6

The night was cool. Dinner, which consisted of stewed beans, bread, olives, and goat milk, had finished, and the dishes were cleaned and stacked on their low shelves along the walls of the cooking area. The girls were free for a few minutes. Free . . . but it was almost as if their mother were still there, watching them over their shoulders, giving advice whether they wanted it or not, calling them back for another forgotten chore.

But Mother was not there. She had died with Father three months earlier. Fever had struck the village and killed 15 people. Their parents had been two of the unfortunate ones who hadn't been strong enough to fight off the illness. First their father died, and then their mother passed away only four days later. It had seemed that their mother would pull through, but when she heard of her husband's death, it was as if she gave up.

Now the girls—well, not really girls as much as young women— found themselves left to run a home alone. Martha was 16 and Mary 15. Mary was stunningly beautiful—but also daring and dangerous. She took risks that Martha did not like even to think about.

"Mother would tell us to keep our heads covered," Martha said softly.

Mary gave her sister a flat stare.

"You could be seen from the road," Martha added.

"I'm not seen from the road. We are next to our house, under a tarp, and shielded by trees. Besides, it's dusk. Who will be out on the streets at this time? That crippled boy?"

"Crippled boys have mouths too."

"Tell Lazarus I'm visiting Aunt Yardena tonight." Mary picked at the corner of her veil with two fingers.

"Don't fray your veil. We can't get anything new. You know that."

"You aren't Mother!"

"Maybe not, but I'm what you've got!" Martha replied, equally heated.

"Will you tell Lazarus that I'm at Aunt Yardena's or not?"

"Is that where you will be?"

"Will it make you feel better to believe so?" A smile toyed at her lips.

Mary was playing with her life, and all she could see was a joke— one at Martha's expense. Good Martha. Devoted Martha. Obedient

Martha. Martha who was keeping herself pure and good, so that a decent man would want to make her his. One day, such a man would be told what a good cook she was, how clean and neat she was, how orderly and proper. And then he would decide that he wanted her, because she would bring him honor. And they would get married and have a houseful of rambunctious children who would test Martha's patience endlessly.

But who would marry her? Perhaps her cousin, Jacob. He was only five years her senior, and so tall and handsome. It was common for cousins to marry. When a woman must cover herself in public, who else would see her and learn to love her? Marriages between cousins were always encouraged to keep the family wealth embedded firmly in the family. Perhaps Jacob would notice her. Perhaps he would ask his father for her.

"It would make me feel better if you were telling the truth," Martha said, pursing her lips in disapproval. "You think this is a game, but it's not! It's very dangerous!"

"So you insist."

"You've seen a woman stoned."

"No, I haven't."

"Maybe you were too young to remember." Martha thought back. "I only remember it vaguely. We must have been 4 or 5 years old. Maybe younger. But she was stoned. Right here in our village."

"I don't remember it." Mary looked sulky.

"It was terrible. I remember the rocks hitting her. I remember her crying and trying to get away from them. Someone pushed her back into the circle. There is no getting away when the village wants you dead. Then someone took a large stone and hit her in the head for the final blow. Mother told me it was her own brother!"

"Don't tell me these things! It's horrible!"

"It will be you if you aren't careful!" Martha replied, leaning forward intently. "It will be you!"

"And you'd throw the first stone, wouldn't you, Martha?"

Her sister looked away in anger. So pretty, but so stupid! Why couldn't she see?

"It wouldn't be me anyway," Mary declared.

"And what makes you so special?"

"I'm not married!" Mary said with a laugh. "I'm not dishonoring any husband. Who else cares enough to stone a woman? Lazarus? He'd never! He's just a little boy! Father might have . . . but he's dead. So with no husband or father to dishonor, what does it matter about appearances?"

"Do you ever want a husband?"

"You do. You want Jacob."

"Maybe I do!"

"Well, I'll marry a rich man," Mary continued. "I'll be his fourth wife, and he won't care what I do! He'll dress me in purple and give me perfume and oils . . . Perfume that would cost more than your husband was worth!"

"A rich man has more honor to lose than a poor man," Martha said.

Mary sniffed and turned her face away, her eyes looking suddenly worried. She was still very young. Martha looked at her with a mixture of protectiveness and jealousy. Her sister was beautiful. That too-wide mouth of hers had matured into a dazzling smile. The funny, mousy eyes were now large and expressive. The twiggy little body had grown into a voluptuous woman. Men wanted her.

"You're worrying," Martha commented.

"I'm not," Mary replied, veiling her thoughts behind a serene expression once more.

"What if Lazarus asks Aunt Yardena if you were there?"

"He won't. He's just a boy, even though he thinks he's so grown-up. What does he know of these things, little Lazarus? Besides, Uncle Simon will say I was there."

"Why should he?" Martha demanded.

"He just will." Mary turned a too-grown-up gaze onto her older sister. "Trust me there."

Was it still happening? Martha had thought that it had stopped! Was Uncle Simon still . . . ? She shuddered.

"Mary . . ."

The girl was silent.

"Is our uncle . . . ?" Not finishing the question, she just looked at her sister's face. Mary's expression became stony. Her mouth broke into a smile, but her eyes flashed something different—something harder and angrier, like shards of pottery.

"Our family is a close and protective unit, is it not?" she asked, spitting out the words with venom. "Our family takes care of itself. Keep it in the family, right? Keep the money, the property . . . Keep the love in the family!"

"Oh . . ." Martha breathed. She should have known sooner—shouldn't have been so naive! But what could she do? Was her sister blackmailing her uncle for past sins, or was his support her payment for his present ones?

Martha could feel the corners of her mouth turning down in disgust. She loathed him! If anyone should be stoned, it was *he*! So oily and smooth. So proud as the patriarch of their family. Stealing the very soul of his own niece . . .

"I hate him," Martha whispered.

"Hate him all you like," Mary said, standing and shielding her eyes to look beyond the trees to the path that led by their house. "It won't change a thing. Use him! That's the secret! Use the stupid old man for every favor you can squeeze out of his old hairy body."

Martha's eyes widened, and then narrowed as she looked at her sister, straining to see through the darkening dusk. Such filthy words coming out of such a young woman . . . out of her own sister! For all she hated her uncle, she was beginning to dislike her sister.

"That's my sign," she said, looking back with a flirtatious wink. "I'll be back later on tonight. Don't worry about me! And remember, tell our brother, if he doesn't believe I'm in bed, that I'm with Aunt Yardena!"

Mary pulled her veil up around her head, her face disappearing in the folds of dark fabric. Then she looked carefully in both directions. Lazarus had already fallen asleep inside the house. He always did. After working hard all day in the fields, he dropped asleep as soon as his stomach was filled. But Mary peered around anyway before she dashed off, running the way small girls do, jumping over rocks and hoisting up their skirts. It reminded Martha of years ago, when a much smaller Mary with her wide mouth and staring eyes had looked breathlessly at her older sister and said, "Martha! We'd better not get caught!"

"Oh, God!" Martha whispered. "Don't let her get caught!"

That night Martha lay in her sleeping area. Lazarus slept flat on his back, his mouth open, snoring loudly. He had not stirred since he lay down after his dinner. He would wake before dawn, however. Quickly adjusting to their father's routine, he was the man of the house now, despite his downy beard, barely starting to grow in, and his boyishly thin chest, not quite filled out to manly proportions. And Martha would have been up for an hour already, preparing his morning meal and packing a lunch for him.

They slept in different rooms. Lazarus had the chamber their parents used to occupy. Not long ago, they all used to line their mats up side by side, the three of them. But now things were different. They weren't the three children anymore. One of them was expected to be a man, and the other two would hopefully be married off soon. It felt like playing house—the way Martha used to imagine she was a married woman taking care of her own home when her mother would leave her in charge and go to visit a neighbor for a few hours in the afternoon. But it wasn't playing anymore. She wasn't pretending—she was mistress of this house. The running of the home was her responsibility.

Martha should have been sleeping. If she didn't want to drag around the next morning like a wet fleece, she needed her sleep. It would be only a few hours before she would have to wake up again and begin another day of chores. Mary wasn't much help around the house as it was, and it was all Lazarus could do to keep up his strength to do the work of a full-grown man. Not that men helped around the house anyway. But she felt the responsibility to care for him.

A twig snapped outside. Mary was back. Lazarus' snores sputtered, then continued. That boy had always slept like a stone. Martha held her breath and waited. Only silence greeted her. Pushing back her cover, she crept to the door. Slipping past her snoring brother, she eased the front door open, wincing against the scraping of the wooden door against the earthen floor, and stepped outside into the night. As she shivered against the cold, she pulled her robe closer around her.

"Mary?" she whispered.

She received no answer, but she could hear some snuffling coming from the side of the house. Martha crept forward and stopped when she saw the hunched form of her sister sitting in the dirt, her back against the plastered wall of the house. Her veil had fallen back, and her hair was tousled and had a leaf sticking out from under a curl. Mary's hair looked dusty, and she kept clenching her hands into fists and pounding them against her knees in a steady rhythm.

"Mary?" Martha repeated softly.

"I hate myself," her sister whispered between choked sobs. "I . . . I . . . hate . . ." She stopped and just sat there, trying to control her breathing.

Martha sank down next to her sister and took one of Mary's clenched fists between her hands.

"What did you do?"

"What do you think I did?" Mary turned her red-rimmed eyes toward her older sister.

"Why did you do it?"

"He said I was beautiful."

"You are beautiful," Martha said quietly.

"He wanted me."

"It is still a sin against God and the family." Bitterness crept into her voice.

"I know." Tears squeezed from under Mary's wet lashes. "And I hate myself."

"What happened here?" Martha asked, pulling up Mary's sleeve, exposing a deep purplish bruise. Her sister inhaled sharply when Martha touched the spot.

"It was when I asked . . ." Mary stopped, her eyes turning hard again like broken pottery.

"What did you ask for?" Martha asked gently.

"I asked for my payment." She pulled her robe down to cover the bruise.

"And he hurt you?"

"He kicked me," she whispered.

Rage swept through Martha. Blind fury. Who would allow a girl to degrade herself, then kick her like a wild dog? Who would take advantage of someone like Mary, even if she did offer herself?

And just as quickly the rage turned from the unknown man toward her sister. Her sister. A prostitute! A whore! Selling herself to God knew whom for a little money. What did she need with money? Their father had left the entire estate to Lazarus, and they lived quite comfortably. They had no needs—well, not monetary needs, at least. And here, Martha's younger sister, would sneak out at night in order to sleep with men about the village. For what? What was the purpose? Simply to degrade herself and fornicate like a wild animal?

"You hate me too," Mary said, wiping the tears from her face.

"I don't hate you."

"I can see it in your eyes. You hate me."

"You are a prostitute." Martha could hear the sound in her voice as she said the words. "A whore. A woman of disrepute. You are the kind of woman that the rest of us whisper about and shun in the market. My sister!"

"I'm not!"

"What do you call it, then?"

Mary did not answer.

"You are a prostitute, and people will know!" Martha's voice rose as she began to feel hysterical. "They'll know, Mary! We'll be ruined! You'll never get married! Our family will be shamed!"

Shaming was the worst punishment. You could never change the community's perception of you. They would always regard it as the truth. Your shame became like a brand. Sister of the prostitute. Brother of the prostitute. Others would always wonder where your family had failed in order to produce such a woman. And if the family had produced one whore, perhaps the other just hid her behavior more successfully! Their family would always be the family of the prostitute. Nothing could change or erase it. Not unless . . .

The thought was unthinkable. But it was true. Not unless the shamed member of the family was duly punished. Not unless the family stood up and threw the offending member from them—allowing her to receive punishment as the village saw fit. Then, and only then, would the community choose to forget. Because then, and only then, would the village see that the family did not condone such atrocity.

And the punishment for adultery? Stoning. Martha shuddered.

"They must never know!" Martha whispered fiercely. "Never!"

Mary looked mutely at her.

"And you must promise me never to do this again!"

The younger girl still did not speak.

"Come to bed," Martha ordered.

As they tiptoed back into the house, Martha glanced back at her sister, and she saw, under the womanly body, the little girl. The little girl who had grown into a common whore.

How had this happened to their family?

Not far away stood the house of Uncle Simon. In it slept their uncle and aunt. And also sleeping somewhere nearby them was Jacob. Jacob—her heart lurched at the thought of him. So manly and handsome, he confronted the world with the pride of a prince. One day she hoped he would look in her direction and see something other than a bossy young cousin. She wanted him to see her as a woman . . . as a wife . . .

Did he know about Mary? Oh, she prayed not! She prayed that he'd never guess! She prayed that he'd somehow miss the signs and still develop a yearning for his dead uncle's eldest daughter. More than just a good wife to him, she would love and adore him. If he would let her, she would be everything to him . . .

The cool night breeze blew against Martha's arms, and she shivered, pulling herself indoors as quietly as she could.

Oh, God, what is my future? she prayed. *What will ever become of me? Oh, please, please, give me to Jacob . . .*

CHAPTER 6

"There is nothing concealed that will not be disclosed, or hidden that will not be made known."

LUKE 12:2

It was strange how a prostitute seen on the street could be glared at, spit at, and ignored as if she were a stray dog. But when that prostitute is your sister . . . when you remember her as a child

. . . when you share your meals with her, and try to help her hide the truth lest someone find out and the family be ostracized, or worse, your sister be stoned to death in the center of a furious circle of villagers . . . everything is different then. Yes, you judge and despise her. But under it all you can't help loving her still. And loving her is the most painful part. You wish that you could hate her totally! That she would go away and never come back. But you don't want her to be stoned—killed by cruel rocks being flung mercilessly at her head, her eyes wide with terror and pain. No, that is too much for you to take. Let her leave, instead, and let you try to forget her, comforted somehow with the knowledge that somewhere she must be alive.

And if she returns? Even if she has somehow reformed? Sometimes she unknowingly carries with her other feelings she didn't know she would bring, like burrs stuck to the hem of her robes . . .

Secrets. Their family was filled with them . . . choked with them until they could not breathe past the lump of secrets that stuck in their chests. And now, with Uncle Simon dying, it felt as if those secrets were too much to bear.

It was morning again. And Martha was back, helping her aunt cook for the guests who kept coming to pay their respects. Martha sat cutting the cucumbers into small pieces to mix with spices, olives, and oil. The kitchen area was already hot, the fire burning high as a mutton stew boiled. Some important people would be here this day—wealthy people. They deserved meat. The savory broth already filled the courtyard with its rich, meaty aroma, and Martha's stomach growled. She hadn't eaten properly this morning. Her mind was too busy, and now her body reminded her of her negligence.

"He is most definitely dying," Lazarus had told her that morning. "He won't last more than a few days. If you saw him . . . He's so weak and helpless, like a little child again. Poor man. But he has lived a good life! He will rest in God!"

Martha had not commented. A good life was something very foreign to Uncle Simon, and she knew it. Only Lazarus seemed to be fooled, always believing the best in someone, because it was more comfortable that way. Her brother had always believed the best in

Mary, too, refusing to see what she was really up to. But then, he had been only a boy, at the beginning. And what one closes his eyes to as a boy oftentimes remains invisible as he grows older. It took several years for the truth to dawn on him. Martha had not aided him in the discovery, but watched him dispassionately as the various details came together in his head. When they did, he was hurt and furious, not knowing what to do.

But that was years ago. In the here and now Lazarus firmly believed that his uncle was a holy man.

"Martha, pass me the dill," Aunt Yardena said. "And the salt, please."

Martha did as bid, and watched as her aunt expertly measured out the dried weed in her hand before dropping it into the simmering pot. Aunt Yardena's face had aged during the past day. Her eyes were sad, and the lines around her mouth and eyes were much more pronounced. Even her hair had lost its silver luster, looking faded and limp. Yet she kept cooking and cooking and cooking . . . never stopping. Never pausing to rest herself or her mind. It was all Aunt Yardena knew how to do—her only way to deal with what was happening to her family.

The sweat stood out on her aunt's brow, and Martha wiped at the moisture on her own forehead. It was hot. She had flung her veil to the side some time ago, as it kept slipping off her shoulders and dangling into the food. Martha knelt before a wooden plank, cutting and dicing, her fingers knowing the work better than her mind did. The grit from the earthen floor ground into her knees, and she sat back for a moment, stretching her back.

Her cousins, Shiloh and Tisha, had stopped their work and were talking quietly in a corner, sitting cross-legged. Martha did not blame them. While they still had things to do, it seemed that it was more of Aunt Yardena's creation than actual need. Their mother was trying to work out her grief, and the young women did not feel that need. Shiloh and Tisha had labored all morning, and now the sun was quite high in the sky.

Mary, who had accompanied Martha this morning to their uncle's home, was grinding grain slowly in a stone basin that rose up out of the ground. A stone embedded naturally in the earth, it was perfectly situated for grinding, and therefore had not been removed when the house was built. Likely the stone that they saw was only the tip of a mammoth boulder beneath the surface—much like the appearance the family displayed to the public.

Her expression serene and quiet, she worked methodically, her body rising and falling with the motion of the grinding stone. Back and forth. Back and forth. Her mind seemed to be flowing elsewhere, somewhere far away. Martha watched her for a moment, then turned back to her own work.

"Woman! Wife!"

The voice from the sleeping area was less forceful today. Aunt Yardena looked up quickly and wiped her hands on a rag. Her sandals slapped softly against the earthen floor as she slipped away. She wasn't gone for long, reemerging only a few moments later.

"Martha," she said, her voice wooden. "Your uncle is calling for you."

Her niece looked up in surprise.

"Martha?" Shiloh said, her voice sarcastic. "Whatever for?"

"I don't know," Aunt Yardena said quietly. "But he asked for her."

"I will go," Martha said, pushing herself to her feet. Her knees ached as she rose, and it felt good to stretch her legs.

"Perhaps he's being kind," Tisha whispered, loud enough to be overheard. "Poor Martha . . . no one to want her in this village . . . she doesn't have the honor of a husband and children as we do."

Although Martha felt the heat rise in her face, she pointedly ignored her cousin and walked toward the sleeping area where her uncle lay.

The room was dark and stank of sweat and sickness. The air was thick, and left a bad taste in her mouth. Swallowing quickly, she forced herself to breathe through her nose so as not to taste the air. Her uncle lay on a mat on the far side of the room. He wasn't the same large man she had known all her life. He was much smaller now—emaciated by his illness. His face was gray, and his hair was sweaty and stringy. His big hands lay lifelessly over his stomach, and he turned large sunken eyes toward her. The change in him startled her. Not having physically seen her uncle during the past month, she was shocked at his condition.

"Martha," he said in a quiet voice.

She stopped at the door, looking down at her leather sandals uncomfortably.

"Come closer. It tires me to speak so loudly."

Yet he still managed to shout for his wife. As she smiled to herself she hoped that it caused him great pain to do it.

"Still my little Martha," Uncle Simon said, misinterpreting her smile.

Crossing the room, she squatted next to his mat. With a heavy sigh he lifted one big hand with considerable effort. She made no move to touch him. He let it drop once more.

"You are grown now."

"Yes, Uncle."

"And not married yet."

"No, Uncle."

"Why not?"

"I should ask you," she said bitterly. Her uncle, the man who stood in the place of her dead father, should have found her a match. If Lazarus could not, her uncle should have fulfilled his duty!

"Ah, well, my dear, you are not so easy to match," he said, then coughed heavily and spat some mucus into a bowl beside him. The stench from the bowl nauseated her.

"Don't worry about that now," she said. Her brother had found her a husband. Jebuseh. She would be a wife yet, and with no help from the old man. It was better this way. Martha would rather be thankful to her brother than her uncle.

He gave a low laugh.

"You are comfortable unmarried? You like it?"

She was silent.

"This family is a family with honor. It should remain so."

"Yes, Uncle."

Sighing and closing his eyes, he lay so still that he looked almost dead. After a few moments she rose to her feet.

"Don't go," he said in a whisper. She froze. What did he want from her?

"Do you need something, Uncle? Water? Are you hungry?"

"No, I need nothing," he said bitterly. "But I want to tell you something."

"What is that?"

"You are difficult to match for a reason, and you must know it."

Martha sighed. She knew much more than she should about her family. "I don't need to hear it, Uncle. You should rest."

"You will hear it!" he said more forcefully. "You are stubborn. You cook, yes, but you are cold and unmoving. You have no passion. You arouse no passion. Ugly women can be married quite easily. It is not your face that holds you back from marriage."

She said nothing.

"You should know it. As a man, I can sense what other men would see—what they see in you. You are like an uncooked fish, Martha."

"And Mary is not?" Martha snapped.

"Mary?" he asked with a low chuckle. "No, for all the things she is, she is not cold!"

Martha had to grip her hands tightly to keep from lashing out at the old man. They were his nieces! His conduct toward Mary was forbidden by God!

"Perhaps I did not want your notice," she managed to say after a moment. "Perhaps I wanted to be unappealing to you, Uncle."

The old man opened his eyes and looked at her with glittering alertness.

"And why is that? You can tell a dying man, can you not?"

"You know what I speak of," she answered in a low voice.

"I know nothing," he said, closing his eyes once more.

"Well, I do," she hissed, glaring down at him with unveiled dislike. "You broke her, Uncle. She didn't need to become what she did!"

"You blame a woman's weakness on a man of my stature?" he asked in disbelief.

"I put the blame where it is due," she replied coldly. "I know what you did to her."

"Jealous," he said was a low laugh. "She was pretty and you were not."

"She was a child! And you were her protector!"

"I know nothing of what you speak."

She should leave now—she knew it. Should walk out and not pursue the matter. But it was filling her, rising like water in a jug. And he lay there, so weak and helpless. The man who had damaged them beyond forgiveness! The man who had molested her sister—raped Mary as a child—and ruined her! The man who had held Martha back, told her how ugly she was, and never permitted her to marry!

"Your sin will not be unnoticed by God," Martha said quietly. "You will answer to Him for what you've done!"

"I have no sin to confess."

"You do." She leaned closer. "I saw you, Uncle."

He froze.

"I saw it." Slowly she repeated the words.

"Well, maybe you did," he said, opening his eyes again. "But what does God care about women? Nothing. Men are his servants. Women are only wombs. And you are not even that, Martha."

"I am right with God. Are you, Uncle?"

The old man let out another low laugh.

"Children do not understand what is really happening around them," he said after a moment. "And prostitutes lie. So what is it that you want? What would you have me do for you? Obviously you want something to be telling me such garbage."

"Nothing. I want nothing. Your power is finished."

"Such a mouth on a woman!" he said, disgust dripping from his tone. "I am not dying yet, girl. And if you open that ugly mouth of yours again, I will ruin the rest of your life. I will stop you from ever marrying, even after my death! I will keep you childless and lonely. You think I cannot do it? I am a man with power and influence. The words of an influential man go far, girl."

Martha just stared at him.

"Get out," he hissed.

Rising to her feet, she walked evenly out of the room. Behind her she could hear the ragged breathing of the old man as he pushed himself up once more to cough heavily and spit into the bowl.

"I am a good man," she heard him wheeze before she was gone. "A holy man. God will reward my good deeds. I have no sin to confess."

Whom was he talking to? Was it to her? to himself? to God?

"What did Father want?" Shiloh asked, her tone more respectful this time.

"To wish me well," Martha answered.

"You were gone for a long time," Tisha said reproachfully.

"He was concerned about my unmarried state."

"Hmm." Aunt Yardena nodded. "We all are, dear."

As Martha looked away, Mary caught her eye, and Martha exchanged a glance with her sister. Mary knew what had happened. Somehow she sensed it.

"She will marry," Mary said quietly.

"Perhaps she will," Tisha replied with a laugh. "You will not, though!"

Mary said nothing.

"Oh, leave her alone," Shiloh interrupted. She put her hands on her plump hips and shook her head. "It is not a time for fighting!"

"No, it is a time for family," Tisha agreed. "And she is no family of mine."

"I will leave," Mary said quietly.

"Please do!" Tisha snapped. "You should have felt the need to leave much earlier. Forcing me to say it was wrong on your part!"

"This is not right!" Martha said suddenly.

"She's a whore!" Tisha snapped. "You have no husband to protect!"

"I was forgiven," Mary said, almost too quietly to hear. They all turned and stared at her. Forgiven? Who could forgive her? What did it matter who had forgiven her if her family did not?

"You can hate me. But I am not the same woman. Jesus forgave me. He showed me what I could be. He took away my sin." Her voice was quivering with emotion, and Martha looked away uncomfortably. Why did Mary always have to do this? Why did she have to become so embarrassingly passionate?

"Jesus?" Tisha demanded. "A wandering, homeless preacher!"

"A healer, a miracle worker," Mary said, turning toward her cousin. "And He forgave me!"

"And what does that do for you?" Tisha sneered.

"You may not love me. But One does. I am loved. I have value in heaven." Mary stood, her chin held high and her eyes flashing. "I have value, cousin! I am not the whore I used to be! I am a woman, just like you. I have been forgiven. You could be forgiven too!"

"For what, pray tell?" Tisha laughed. "I have been honorable. I have not committed adultery!"

"We all have something, don't we?" Mary asked meaningfully.

Martha suddenly grabbed her sister's arm and wheeled her around.

"Thank you for your hospitality, Aunt," Martha said evenly. "But we must go."

Ducking her head, Mary allowed herself to be steered out the door. Martha stomped along next to her sister, her emotions raging. The sun was high, and Martha felt her head swimming in the heat. It was a surprisingly hot day, and she had not been prepared for it.

"What is wrong with you!" Martha suddenly shouted to her sister. "Why are you the way you are?"

"What am I?"

"You an embarrassment! You are self-righteous when you have no right to be!" Martha spat out. "You preach at people! You have no proper shame! You come back here after being gone for four months and think that everyone will forget what you did to our family! You didn't have to be a prostitute! I didn't!"

"I cannot change what I've done," Mary said. "But I am a changed woman."

"Changed or not, you still move in the world of men. You act like a man. You talk like a man. You are forward and speak out of turn. You show too many emotions all of the time. You might as well discard your veil for all the good it does you!"

"How can I be part of the world of women when they shun me?" Mary demanded. "Women will never accept me again. What am I to do? How am I to act? Whom am I to talk to?"

"Frankly, I don't care. I just don't care." Suddenly Martha felt drained. Turning, she walked away, her steps slow and heavy. Angry and exhausted from her anger, she was tired of being the good one. Tired of the embarrassment, of shouldering the shame that her sister had brought on them. And every time she thought she could cut her sister out of her life and forget her, her heart would suddenly remind her that Mary was her sister and that she loved her.

Love was exhausting. But then hate was exhausting too. It was easier not to care, if that were possible at all.

CHAPTER 7

"Therefore be as shrewd as snakes and as innocent as doves."

MATTHEW 10:16

The morning was already hot. The heat rose from the dusty ground in visible waves that distorted the whole world. The mountainside was a drab-brown color, with patches of pale-green where the olive groves flourished. But at this time of year, flourishing was an overstatement. It was hot and dry, and the trees survived by plunging deep into the ground for any moisture they could find. Their leaves drooped, just like the people who tended them. Martha shaded her eyes and leaned momentarily against the doorjamb. Tugging at her veil, she tucked a stray tendril of hair out of her eyes.

Out in one of those olive groves, Jacob was working alongside Uncle Simon. Jacob would be telling the day laborers what to do. At the end of the day he would help his father to measure out the payment. Now he would be standing tall and glistening in the hot morning sun. She sighed, letting her mind wander over her handsome cousin's attributes.

"Are you still sweeping, Martha?" her mother asked.

Turning back to her job, Martha pulled the broom of dried grass across the packed dirt floor. The inside of the house was remarkably cooler, but also almost dark compared to the outside brightness. She rubbed her eyes.

"Shut the door, Martha," her mother reminded her, and the girl closed the rough wooden door. "Keep the heat outside."

"Where is Lazarus?" Martha asked.

"With the other boys," her mother replied. "He'll be back in time for his lunch. He always is!"

"H'mm."

"Don't sound like that! A man's life is hard enough when he grows up. He must provide an income for his family and shelter and protect a household. Let him play while he can."

"I didn't complain."

"You are learning to be a good wife. A wise wife works hard. She doesn't lounge about and let her home go to ruin. And she takes care of her men."

Martha felt a little surge of pride. She was taking care of her men, too. Her father and her brother were her men, were they not? Thus she belonged to them, and they belonged to her. She was doing the job of a good woman.

"Will a man want to marry me?"

"Of course! Men don't want just a pretty face, you know. A man wants a woman who can take care of the home and face life with pride and courage. Any pretty face can let everything fall around her. Any pretty face can melt into a puddle at the sight of hard work!"

"I want to get married," Martha said matter-of-factly.

"You are too young still," her mother chuckled. "You are only 12. A few years more, my dear. Don't rush it!"

"Will I be pretty?"

"What a silly question!" Her mother laughed. "God gave every woman beauty. You don't need to try at it like a pagan. No painting and elaborate braids for you, Martha! Beauty comes from your heart."

"Will I marry my cousin?"

"It is hard to tell yet. It would be a good to have a close kin union, to be sure, but your uncle is a strange man."

Martha knew her mother would not say anything more on the subject. It was not her place to insult her husband's brother. But obvious distrust existed between the houses. Still, Jacob was a handsome boy. Already 17, he was strong and nicely built. As for Martha, she spent her hours of hard work thinking about him, her mind filled with images of those strong arms, already laboring alongside his father in overseeing the olive groves. If he were her husband, she thought that she would be the happiest girl ever! And if their betrothal were arranged, she would never complain again about anything. She would work like a donkey!

"Silly girl," her mother chuckled, seeming to read her mind. "You have no idea what marriage is, do you?"

"What is it, then?"

But her mother wouldn't say anything more. Instead she turned her back on her daughter and hummed a tune to herself, lifting the water jug to pour some of the precious contents into a basin.

"Mary!" her mother called.

Silence. "Mary!" she said a bit louder, listened, then shook her head and clucked her tongue in disapproval.

"Wasn't she outside gathering sticks?" Martha asked.

"She should be back by now." Their mother was a tall, strongly built woman with small eyes and gray-streaked hair. Her attractive features were now slightly worried.

"I could go find her," Martha offered.

"That child." Her mother shook her head again. "That hard head of hers will either be her downfall or her greatest strength!"

"She never does her share," Martha muttered.

"Go find her," her mother said, waving her hand. "I will finish here."

Martha dropped her broom with a clatter and dashed out the door. Freedom! Annoyed with her sister, Martha was jealous that the younger girl got to play more than she did. At 12, Martha was nearly a woman, but there was also a child inside of her that had not yet faded into the background.

She knew where to find her sister. Mary had a favorite hiding place behind the house. When she needed to be alone, the girl would sit next to a fig tree, its broad, wilting leaves providing shade. And if she picked just the right place, a dip in the ground that she nearly disappeared into, and pulled up her dusty veil, she was nearly invisible.

Like a desert rat, Martha thought to herself.

"Mary!" Martha whispered, looking behind her carefully so as not to be seen. It would be cruel to give away her sister's hiding spot. Besides, if she found a new one, how would Martha find her when she needed to? "Mary, it's me!"

Martha stopped short when she saw her little sister's tear-stained face. It was ashen, and her lips were quivering. Her large eyes were wider than ever, and she clamped one hand over her wide mouth to stifle a sob.

"Mary, what happened?" Martha asked, sinking to the ground beside her. "What's wrong?"

The girl just put her head down on her knees and cried, her slender shoulders heaving with her tears.

"Tell me, Mary." Martha pulled her upright. "It can't be so bad."

"I'm dying," her sister whispered.

"Nonsense! If you can cry like this, you are not near death."

Mary sniffled. Martha's logic had a way of snapping her out of dramatic circumstances every time.

"It's true, though," Mary went on, trying to get hold of herself. "It's only a matter of time."

"And what are you dying of?"

"I'm . . ." Her eyes filled with new tears, and she covered her face with her hands.

"You're what?" Martha asked, removing her hands from her face. "What?"

"I'm smitten by God!"

"By God? How?"

"I'm . . ."

Mary seemed unable to say it. But she produced a rag covered in blood. Martha looked at it in horror, and then back at her sister.

"Where are you bleeding?" Martha gasped. "I'll get Mother! But where?"

"I'm evil." Mary's voice gained strength. "It happened because of my wickedness!"

Martha could feel the panic welling up inside of her. Her sister had always been dramatic by nature, but this time, it seemed, she had something legitimately wrong with her, and it terrified Martha to the core. She glanced anxiously back toward the dusty walls of the house, mentally calculating how long it would take her to run around to the front, rush through the door, and fetch her mother.

"Don't tell Mother!" Mary wailed, seeming to sense her sister's intent. "Please, I can't bear for her to know!"

"What if you die?" Martha whispered.

"Then bury me here!" Mary exclaimed, waving around them.

"Mary, stop this!" Martha grabbed her sister by the shoulders and shook her hard. "Stop this now!"

Clamping her mouth shut, Mary stared mutely at her.

"Tell me what happened. Stop talking of dying."

"It's because I'm so wicked. It's because of my sin!" Tears started flowing again, and Martha released her grip on her sister's shoulders in exasperation.

"It happened all of a sudden," Mary whispered. "When Uncle took me aside. It happened then."

"You began to bleed?" Martha asked carefully.

"Because of what Uncle did!" Mary said, her eyes filled with horror. "God is punishing me for what Uncle did!"

"Where are you bleeding from?" Martha asked, her eyes narrowing shrewdly.

Mary was silent for several moments, chewing the inside of her cheek. Finally she leaned forward. Martha put down her head, and Mary whispered the place in her ear, her face turning red in embarrassment. She had a pained, tense expression on her face, like a servant waiting to be slapped.

Suddenly Martha nodded in understanding. "You are not dying. You are becoming a woman, that's all."

Her sobs drying up at the matter-of-fact tone of Martha's words, Mary looked sideways at her sister. "But what about what Uncle did?" she asked in shock.

"That is something else altogether."

And so Martha explained what all girls must hear for a first time. She told about children and babies being born, about a woman's body, and about how a girl turns into a woman, and one day passes through a rite of passage that recurs once each month. Something that must be endured . . . a secret to be kept . . .

But what about their uncle? Martha knew now what she had suspected all along. She realized what he was doing to Mary.

"Mary," Martha whispered. "Mother told me that God listens to the prayers of a wife—that a good wife can put her petitions before God and be heard . . ."

"Yes?" Mary seemed a little confused.

"Soon," her sister said, her voice low and insistent, "I will be old enough to marry. And a man will want me to be his. He will arrange it with Father, and then he will come for me. And when he does . . . when I become a wife . . ."

The younger girl's eyes grew large, and she held her breath with the sheer importance of the speech.

"What then?"

"Then I will pray to God. As a wife, I will pray to God that He will kill Uncle Simon!"

Mary gasped.

"I will! I will pray that God will kill him as He did the Philistines! Because I think Uncle Simon is even more wicked than the Philistines! I will pray, never for myself, and always for this! I promise it!"

The girls looked solemnly into each other's eyes.

"And Mary," Martha said softly. "If you see him, run away! Don't listen to him speak! Don't obey! Run away!"

"Isn't that very wicked too?" Mary asked in disbelief.

"I think so. But I think Uncle is more wicked than a disobedient girl."

That evening, after they had washed the supper dishes and covered the leftover food and put it aside, Martha and Mary stayed in the kitchen storage area with their mother. Their father was talking with Uncle Simon. The oil lamp was burning low, and Martha leaned against her mother's strong arm, watching the shadows flicker against the walls. The orange glow of the weakening lamp illuminated the tall clay jars that lined the opposite wall. Near their bases, each one bore a stamp—the sign of the potter who made it. They were all the work of their mother's second cousin. He gave them a special price. Hanging above the pots were some herbs, drying upside down, twined together with string. And piled high, furthest from the fire and the oven, were some sacks of grain and meal. It was a familiar sight, those walls. The pots and herbs and lines of dishes comforted her. Symbols of stability, they kept everything together as it should be. They called their father home again after a hard day of work.

"What do the men say?" Martha asked, looking toward the curtained doorway that led to the living area where they were talking in low tones.

"It is not for women to hear," her mother replied.

"I want to go see Father," Mary piped up.

"You must not, unless he calls you." Her mother's voice sounded tired.

"Don't be stupid," Lazarus said sleepily from his spot next to the fire. "Girls can't go be with men!"

"But I want to," Mary said sullenly.

"And I want a caravan of camels!" he teased. "What do you want, Martha?"

"Stop it," she said irritably.

Lazarus rolled his eyes.

"Go to bed now, children," their mother said. "It is late. And dawn will not come any later just to please you!"

Martha stood and glanced toward her sister. Mary sat on a woven palm frond mat, her back against a bag of grain. Her veil hung down around her shoulders, and she looked defiantly back.

"I'm going to see Father," she announced.

Their mother sighed. Shaking her head, she turned her back on her younger daughter. She didn't believe Mary would do anything of the kind.

But her daughter rose to her feet, gave her a defiant look, and pushed past the curtain that separated the storage area from the living area where the men were talking. It all happened so quickly that Martha's mouth dropped open in shock, and she stared at her mother, who appeared equally alarmed. What Martha knew, and her mother did not, was that Mary had started her menses. Ceremonially unclean, she dared not go near the men and make them unclean! They would not know it, so perhaps God would overlook it, but she knew.

"That child!" her mother hissed, and she marched after the girl. Martha, after an indecisive pause, followed her mother.

Lazarus stayed safely in the kitchen area, but peered out from behind the curtain.

"Father, I thought you called me," Mary said innocently, looking at him with her wide eyes. She was slender, and nearly as tall as a woman, but with a decidedly childlike look about her.

Their father looked up at her from the place where he lounged on the floor next to their uncle. He was obviously weighing the truth of her words.

"Mary, you were not called!" their mother said. "Come back to the kitchen at once!"

"Or was it you, Uncle, who called?" Mary asked brazenly, turning her full stare on the man.

"Not I, child. You are where you don't belong."

Something passed from Mary to Uncle Simon. Something uncomfortable. He squirmed and sat up, looking angry. The blanket beneath him was wrinkled and was piling up on one side of him, leaving one of his legs on the dirt floor. He jerked at the woolen blanket, and Martha heard the fabric squeak under the tension. It would tear with one more tug like that.

"Mary, go to bed," their father said, his tone low and dangerous. "You have done wrong."

"No, no," Uncle Simon said, forcing a tight smile. "Let the girls stay. I like to see my nieces." He wrenched the fabric from under himself and smoothed it with exaggerated gentleness across the floor.

Although their father seemed unconvinced, he gave a slight nod. Mary sat next to her father, sitting with her back straight and her eyes cast down, but her lips were set in a thin, angry line.

Her mother exhaled sharply through her nose, and Martha glanced at her, noticing the anxious expression on her face. Mary was embarrassing their father. By pushing herself into the men's domain, she was acting strangely! What was she doing?

"And Martha?" Uncle Simon asked. "Will you come talk to your uncle?"

Unwillingly she edged closer, giving some one-word replies to his stilted questions, all the while watching her sister.

"I am very tired now," Martha said carefully. "Come, Mary, let us ask our father to allow us to go to bed."

"Please do, girls," he said. His eyes told her that he had not forgotten Mary's indiscretion. Uncle Simon poured the last of the wine into his clay cup, and their mother immediately took the jug and retreated into the kitchen area to fetch more.

Mary pushed herself to her feet and followed her older sister out of the room, her steps slow.

"What have you done?" Martha whispered furiously when they climbed the ladder that led from the kitchen area to the sleeping chamber built onto the roof. "What were you thinking?"

"What will he do?" Mary asked insolently.

"Beat you," Lazarus said angrily, following them into their sleeping chamber. Their mats were already laid out for them, three lined up together.

And Martha suddenly knew that something had changed. Something inside Mary was different now. She had thought things through, deciding that she was not dying and that she was not cursed by God.

"You embarrassed Father!" Martha said. "He'll be very angry with you!"

Saying nothing, Mary took off her robes, leaving on only her tunic. Then she crawled under her cover and rested her head on her bent arm before curling into a tight ball.

"Mary!" Martha exclaimed in frustration. "What is wrong with you?"

"I'm sleeping now," Mary said, closing her eyes.

Lazarus imitated Mary's words, miming her movements flawlessly.

"Oh, stop it, Lazarus!" Martha snapped, and lay down on her own mat.

Today Mary had become a woman. And today everything had changed.

"Did you do that because I teased you?" Lazarus asked after a moment.

"I'm sleeping!" Mary repeated angrily.

"I was just teasing!" Lazarus said, sounding wounded. "I didn't mean for you to do that!"

Mary didn't answer, and Martha could hear their brother brooding silently behind her.

"You shouldn't have teased her," Martha said reproachfully.

It was wrong to blame him, because it had nothing to do with him, she knew. And while the children all lay with their eyes shut on their mats, no one slept.

CHAPTER 8

"For out of the overflow of the heart the mouth speaks."

MATTHEW 12:34

Tying her wide sleeves together behind her back with a firm knot, Rachel then tested her reach. It did not hinder her arms in their movement, and she nodded to herself in satisfaction.

"You are glowing, Rachel!" Shiloh said, smiling at her cousin-in-law, her plump face creasing in good humor. "You are adjusting well to marriage!"

Rachel blushed.

"Life is easy now," Tisha teased, leaning over her shorter sister's shoulder. "Wait till the babies! You'll dream of the easy life you had those first few months of marriage!"

"Bah!" Yardena laughed. "Don't listen to them, Rachel! They forget the difficulties they had adjusting to pleasing a husband. Nothing is harder than those months, and it will only get better, I assure you!"

"Oh, life is not hard!" Rachel said quickly.

"Would you admit to it now?" Yardena asked with a twinkle. "We will talk again in 10 years."

Nervously Rachel glanced around herself. Marriage was difficult. It wasn't pleasing Lazarus that seemed to be the problem, but being pleased herself! Her husband didn't seem to understand the power of his words. Things that he thought were so tiny might have been the Mount of Olives for her! And things that he said only in passing would stab through her heart. How could she stop all of these boiling feelings that raged inside of her? It wasn't his fault. Lazarus was kind and attentive. He provided well and was respectful. It was something inside her that took offense at the least word . . . or was it her? Did he deserve her anger? After all, he never shouted, and she couldn't quite put her finger on what he did. But whatever it was, he did it nevertheless. Never mind trying to change a man! He'd be what he was, she knew that well enough. The only one to change was herself. How could she just learn to be be calm and enjoy being a married woman? How did other women do it, looking so calm and contented? Even Aunt Yardena, with Uncle Simon bellowing at her, seemed to find contentment in the role.

She should be happy, she knew. After all, she was married to a famous man. Not only was he kind and honest, but he had been raised from the dead. It was what people whispered when they heard his name. "Is that the same man who was raised from the dead?" Her husband was special. He was close enough to the Messiah to warrant a special miracle. In fact, he was Jesus' close friend. When Jesus overthrew the Romans, surely Lazarus would receive a high position in the new government! Not many could claim such an intimate connection with an influential man! Lazarus had standing in this village, and stories circulated that he was now immortal and could not die. Lazarus was a husband to be cherished. So why could she not content herself?

But the question faded from her mind as another woman entered the kitchen area. It was Erda, the wife of Jacob.

A woman of average height, Erda had wide hips and a broad smile. She let her veil drop around her shoulders, exposing long, straight hair, with a hint of brown mixed into the black. Although she had a few stray hairs poking out of her chin, overall she had kept herself up well. A small boy clutched at her skirts, staring wide-eyed up at the women.

"Erda!" Yardena exclaimed. "Another child to come?"

The rest of the women looked at Aunt Yardena in perplexity, but Erda only smiled wider.

"Too soon to tell people, but yes, I'm pregnant again!" An explosion of cries of delight and questions that bubbled up like boiling stew instantly greeted her words.

"How did you know, Mother?" Tisha asked, shaking her head.

"A woman who has been pregnant as often as I have been knows these things!" Yardena replied. "I can smell it in the air. I can see it in her skin!"

"But not a word outside this kitchen!" Erda warned with a shaking finger. She unwound the boy's grip on her skirt and allowed Shiloh to tie back her sleeves.

"Enough people pass through this kitchen to make that easy enough!" Shiloh teased. Erda reached back and gave her sister-in-law a playful swat on one of her ample hips.

Rachel looked on in silence. Still new to this family circle, she had not yet become entirely comfortable with them. They were all very nice women, she had to admit, but it would be a few years before she was properly one of them. Maybe it would last until a younger woman, one of their daughters or nieces, married. It was hard to tell. She would be the young, inexperienced one until another entered their ranks. Like Martha, perhaps. Not younger, but she would definitely be more newly married!

"God be with you, Rachel!" Erda said cheerfully. "And how is our new wife?"

"Very well."

"And your appetite?" Erda pressed. "Are you craving olives by the basketful? Are you longing for honey? Do you sleep a lot?"

"Oh, stop!" Tisha laughed. "You should just ask my mother if our Rachel is pregnant and she will tell you straight!"

Rachel looked down uncomfortably. She had no signs yet. At least none that she knew of. It wasn't a subject she liked to be reminded of. If they could give her a secret, share a tip on how to ensure pregnancy, she would gladly accept the information . . . but she dare not ask. She dare not open herself.

"Where is Martha?" Rachel asked, looking around.

"She left," Tisha said, rolling her eyes.

"Left?"

"Mary decided to preach," Shiloh explained. "Martha, mother hen that she always is, hustled her out like a little chick."

Erda made a sound of disapproval with her lips. Her little son kept tugging at her skirts, and she unwound his fingers again. "Go out and play," she said firmly. "Mother is busy now. Go play with the other children."

The boy screwed up his face as if about to wail, but reconsidered after looking at his mother's firm expression. He sat down on his rump and began to make trails in the dirt with his feet.

"I spoil him too much," his mother commented. "He needs to toughen up a little."

The women nodded in agreement. He was a rather whiny child, to be sure. A boy may be his mother's joy, but one who clung to his mother too much would never be a true man. A woman wanted a devoted son, not a dependent son. She wanted to lean on him in her old age, not support an embarrassment. It was a fine balance to be found. As he grew, her son would be her first ally—the one to stand for her and protect her, even against his own father and his father's family. But she must not abuse her son's love for her to his detriment.

"Martha would have made a good wife," Shiloh said.

"But her time is past," Tisha observed, shaking her head sadly. "It won't happen now."

"It might!" Erda said.

"I doubt it," Yardena replied. "We can count on Martha always to be Martha, able in the kitchen and with nothing else to fill her mind."

"Actually . . ." Rachel stopped. Dare she tell? No, it wasn't time to share this news yet. It would be unfair to Martha to give away her secrets.

"Oh, is there news?" Shiloh asked, turning her full attention to her sister-in-law.

"There is; I can see it!" Erda laughed. "Come on, Rachel, out with it!"

"There is our sweet Rachel," Tisha said, putting her arms around the girl's shoulders and pressing their cheeks together. "Good, sweet Rachel. You have to tell us now, you know! You have to!"

"Well," she said with a laugh. "It isn't meant to be spoken of yet."

"Go on, we can keep a secret!" Erda prodded.

"Yes, Rachel, tell us!" Aunt Yardena said with more authority in her voice.

"Well, a marriage is being arranged as we speak. Martha may be married within a few months!"

"No!" Tisha released her hold on Rachel and threw up her hands in shock. "I can't believe it! To whom?"

"Oh, you can't stop there!" Erda pressed. "Who is the man we're losing our Martha to?"

"Jesbuseh!" Rachel said with relish.

"Jebuseh!" Aunt Yardena repeated. "As old as Simon, he is!"

"But wealthy!" Erda pointed out.

"And not bad looking," Shiloh admitted.

"Don't let your husband hear that!" Tisha laughed.

"If he does, I will know who told him!" Shiloh replied.

Yardena frowned. "I don't mind saying that I don't like the thought of Martha being a second wife."

Everyone recognized that what Aunt Yardena really didn't like was the idea of a man her husband's age taking a second wife at all! But any woman could understand that. Not that Yardena had any fear of that now. Her husband was leaving this life, and had no more strength for extra wives.

As the women bantered on in good humor, Rachel groaned inwardly. Lazarus would not be pleased that she had spoken about this. But he also had no idea about the pressure inside a kitchen!

"Too bad it isn't Mary who we're losing to a new mother-in-law," Tisha said with a low chuckle. The other women murmured their agreement.

"There isn't a man stupid enough to take Mary, is there?" Erda asked.

"Oh, hardly!" Rachel assured them.

"If we are made in God's image, then men are not made that stupid," Shiloh added.

"They were dumb enough to hire her services," Rachel pointed out.

"Calling men stupid is not wise," Yardena warned.

The younger women took the hint and blushed a little.

"A prostitute does not find a husband," Yardena went on. "She has nothing to offer anyone that has not been taken already by others."

"Reformed prostitute!" Shiloh added sarcastically.

"So Martha will go to a mother-in-law, and we will be stuck with Mary in our midst!" Tisha said, shaking her head. "Martha might aggravate me something terrible, but Mary is insufferable!"

"Better to keep our eye on her, though," Erda said seriously.

Tisha raised her eyebrows. "By dishonoring us with her presence? No, better that she leave our town altogether!"

Again, there was a hum of agreement.

"Any hope of her leaving, Rachel?" Shiloh asked with a smile.

With a sick smile of her own Rachel shook her head. She had said too much. If Lazarus knew how she'd been talking, he would be hurt. He would pull away from her and stop sharing as much as he did.

But she deserved to be accepted with the women, too! And his whore of a sister had brought enough dishonor! But she'd said too much. Why was she so stupid sometimes? Handing out her household's secrets for a little bit of acceptance!

"Shall we begin cooking?" she asked, her voice weak. "I'd be happy to grind the flour."

"She sounds like Martha," Tisha said, and the women laughed.

Like Martha. No, she sounded like a woman with secrets she was supposed to keep. But now they were all exposed.

Lazarus pushed himself up into a cross-legged seated position. Lounging on one arm, even with a pillow, could get uncomfortable after some time. Several platters scattered about the room contained piles of flatbread, olives, and dried figs. There were bowls of stewed lentils as well and several pitchers of frothy goat milk. A servant girl stood close by the kitchen, waiting to serve. She wasn't very big— maybe 13 at most, with a mousy little face and stringy hair that kept slipping free of her veil. She reminded him a little of Mary at that age—so awkward. It was strange to see how a girl could grow up into a beautiful woman from that stage.

Lazarus turned back to his cousin Jacob, who sat next to him on a tightly woven carpet of many colored stripes. He beckoned for the servant girl, and held up his cup for more wine. She obliged quickly and efficiently.

"Is your father sleeping?" Lazarus asked.

"I believe so. I'll go in to him later and see how he is feeling. Now, he likes to be left alone unless he calls for us, but I don't feel right not at least checking."

"Certainly your mother also checks."

"She does," he nodded. "But Father—well, he doesn't have much patience for women at the best of times!"

Lazarus laughed along at the joke.

As Jacob's face turned more serious, Lazarus felt sorry for him. It was a hard time for any man to lose his father. And while family and friends could help comfort him, the grief would be the same.

"I feel the responsibility for our family more strongly in these uncertain times," Jacob said. "The Romans deal more and more harshly with us, and the young men keep joining bandit bands, only to be crucified in front of their mothers!"

"It's times like these that we used to say, 'God send us the Messiah,'" Lazarus commented with a nod. "But the Messiah has come, and perhaps one day He will overthrow them!"

"Brutal lot." Jacob's lips twisted in distaste. "They are more animal than human in their punishments."

Crucifixion was hideous. The Roman authorities tied their victims to a tall beam and left them to die of exposure. Most often the man would also be whipped before being nailed through his wrists and ankles. The whips had pieces of metal and glass at the ends, so that each lash would rip flesh from the poor victim's back. The only pause came when they waited for him to regain consciousness. What good was torture if the man was not awake to feel it? And then, after all that, with his body shredded and oozing blood, they left him hanging on a cross with the birds of prey settling onto their meal while it still breathed. The position the man was put in made it extremely difficult for him to breathe, so that for each breath he must choose between air, with the agony of pushing himself upward to breathe in, or suffocation. The horrible part was that it would be better for the man to simply suffocate and end his agony, but there was something inside of a human being that longed to breathe, and no matter how excruciating it was, he would do so until he was too weak to struggle anymore. That desperate urge to keep living . . . the terror of not being able to draw another breath . . . it was the cruelest death imaginable.

Why did Jesus keep mentioning it as if the Romans would be capable of killing Him? He was the Messiah! It turned Lazarus' stomach each time Jesus mentioned it.

Several different political currents swept through the land during these uncertain times. To begin with, there were the priests and high religious leaders. They were furious with Jesus for His treatment of them. Jesus labeled them hypocrites. Referring to them as blind and evil, He had accused them of giving the people too many burdens to struggle under so that they could no longer see the beauty of God. Several times He'd called them snakes to their faces. Constantly He'd sidestepped their attempts to trap Him in His own words, so that instead of the people losing confidence in Him, they revered Him more than ever.

The people had always looked to the priests and Pharisees to tell them if they were doing well or not. Simon was a Pharisee. The opinion of the Pharisees was like the measuring stick of a family, telling a person whether they were doing their duty or falling short. Everyone saw themselves through the eyes of the family and village. And people evaluated their spirituality through the eyes of the religious leaders. So when the leaders told them they were breaking the Sabbath or not giving enough to the Temple, they took it seriously. When a Pharisee told you that your child's disfigurement was because of your sin, you believed him. Or when a priest pointed out that your barrenness was because of your evil heart, you accepted the truth of it. And when a leader showed you special regard, you also took that seriously. To be invited to a dinner at a Pharisee's house meant that you were right with God, because the leader had seen your merit. The Pharisees and priests enjoyed their positions of influence and respect. To be called down and told they were doing the people harm filled them with bile. The questioning, uncertain looks in the eyes of the general populace frightened them. One has position only if the community recognizes it. Should the community fail to see your virtue, what are you? Nothing at all.

So the religious leaders had good reason to get rid of Jesus, if He were a regular man vulnerable to their ploys. He was threatening their position by undermining their influence and their honor. More than just planting seeds of doubt in the minds of the people, He was showing them that they did not need the opinion of the priests and Pharisees to indicate whether they were acceptable to God. Jesus jeopardized everything the religious leaders had worked so hard for.

A rabbi studied from the time he was a tiny boy, memorizing the Torah word for word. He learned the complicated laws that hundreds of years of tradition had added to it. Such men spent their lives in books when most people could not even read a word. Regarded as higher than the others, they would give solutions to problems and judge between neighbors. Their village and family viewed them with pride and would never question their intelligence or wisdom. Too many boys had competed for the position of apprentice to the existing rabbis, and to be selected said enough. If a rabbi saw your value, you were valuable indeed. But this Jesus had been a laborer. A commoner. Although He had studied as a boy, He had not continued in the higher learning. Instead, He had worked at His father's craft instead. Yes, He had been an excellent carpenter and stonemason, building houses and providing whatever things made from wood that they needed—and the details were always seen to. The houses Jesus had helped to complete were superbly done. It was work that demanded both skill and muscle.

But to have a carpenter's opinion matter more than a rabbi's? Or to have a stonemason tell a religious leader that he had missed the kingdom of God? It was unheard-of! And when something was that threatening, something must be done. Men with power in the community did not set it down easily, and they would do anything to keep what they had worked so hard to achieve.

Then there was a different current altogether—one that normally flowed in opposition to the Jewish religious leaders. But this time, both currents came together and made a vicious flood. This was the current of Roman politics.

The people had chafed under Rome's direct dominion for three decades now. Rome, of course, saw its own superiority, but convincing the members of the proud Jewish nation of this was difficult.

After all, they were God's chosen people. They did not take well to being subjugated, and stubbornly refused to budge in their customs. Uprisings were frequent. Young men formed bands of brigands, and much of the Jewish community protected them.

"Egypt learned that God's people are not to be enslaved," many said. "Rome will discover that fact as well!"

The Roman Empire gave the Jews grudging respect, but realized that it must either dominate the little nation or see its control over even the surrounding nations begin to unravel. Every major city had a Roman military presence, and soldiers often visited villages that were too small to be of much interest, just to keep their respect. The legionnaires bullied the people, demanding free food and services. They beat the young men who showed disrespect and leered after the village girls like dogs in heat. The Jews hated the Romans. A dead Roman was of no consequence to them.

So when popular opinion circulated that there was a new king of the Jews, the Romans felt the threat. A newly proclaimed king meant that the Jews had not yet accepted Roman rule after all, and were planning further revolt. A new king would inspire the people to oppose Rome even further. The Roman legions must quickly quash him before the people had time to pledge their allegiance, before too much damage was done.

It all came down to politics. And when the sputtering bile of the religious leaders merged with the cold iron of the Roman occupation, the result would be deadly if God did not work a miracle. The king of the Jews . . . the subversive preacher . . . the healer with too much influence . . . if He were a normal man, His death would be sealed! But Jesus was the Messiah. He certainly wouldn't allow them to lay a finger on Him, would He?

This subversive preacher was a special friend to Lazarus. Jesus came to visit him in Bethany in order to rest. They would talk together, and Lazarus would make Him comfortable after too many weeks of dusty travel. He was due to visit again soon, Lazarus knew. He just hoped that Jesus got the message he had sent, and came to heal his uncle.

"The leadership of the family falls to me next," Jacob said, shaking off the political issues that were too heavy for him. "I will have to move into my father's house. I will have to support my mother. I will run the business. And in these uncertain times, I don't mind admitting that I'm nervous. My father was much more influential than I am."

Since he seemed to be talking more to himself than to his cousin, Lazarus did not answer him. Jacob would be taking a great amount of responsibility onto his shoulders upon the death of his father. It was the expected role of the eldest son, but it would not be an easy transition to make.

"You should be thinking of marrying off your sisters, Lazarus," Jacob said suddenly. "I'm not overstepping my bounds and speaking as my father, but rather as your cousin and your friend."

"I know." Lazarus nodded.

"Too many women in a house can be a drain on the resources," Jacob went on. "They do the housework, yes, but how many women do you need for that? You have an able-bodied wife!"

"Marriages are not always so easy to arrange," Lazarus said diplomatically.

"Perhaps not. I do not envy your circumstances. Perhaps a marriage to a poorer man . . . a man without the money to be choosy."

"I'll take care of my sisters." Coldness crept into Lazarus' voice. "I will find them suitable matches."

"I don't mean to offend." Jacob held his hands out as a sign of retreat. "I only mean to give some advice. You haven't got much time."

"Thank you, cousin." Lazarus forced a smile to his face. "I appreciate your concern."

Jacob shrugged and accepted the thanks with a nod. He would be the patriarch of this family. As leader, his advice would be something close to law. Lazarus sighed. While he wanted to please his cousin and have him approve of his decisions regarding his sisters, he also longed for his sisters also to be happy. Furthermore, he desired for the entire family to be happy, but it would require so many different solutions that it was impossible!

Lazarus felt the weight of his burden. He might not be the patriarch, but as the head of his own home he was its leader and responsible for it.

"Do you know what I miss, Lazarus?" another of the men called across the room. "I miss those little honey cakes that your sister makes so well! I can see why you don't marry her off, my friend! Having a cook like that in the house is a great benefit."

The other men laughed aloud, and Lazarus bowed his head to the compliment. Rachel, he was sure, would be beside herself with annoyance at a comment like that, but it would simply have to be a remark he did not repeat around her.

Lazarus beckoned to the servant girl. Quickly slipping to his side, she looked down at her feet respectfully.

"Tell my sister Martha that people are asking for her honey cakes," he said in a low voice. "I'm sure we don't want to disappoint."

"She is not in the kitchen, sir," the girl replied softly.

"Why not?" he demanded, trying to keep his voice low.

The servant looked back blankly. It was not her place to tell the women's business. She would get a swifter punishment from women than she ever would from a man. He sighed and waved her away again.

Deep inside of him he felt anger rising. Ordinarily he was a calm man, but now it coursed up through his body, and he struggled to maintain his composure. Did he not have enough dishonor to deal with, without sisters who refused to act like women? Did he not have enough responsibility without having to remind his unmarried sisters how to behave so as not to shame him? Was he not embarrassed enough that he could not provide husbands? Now it also looked as if he could not command their respect, either!

The man who had made the request politely looked away. His gracious pity was a sharper slap than any direct insult.

But one marriage was almost arranged, he reminded himself. No one knew of it yet, and as long as it stayed . . . discreet . . . until the arrangements were finalized, it would likely go forward without a hitch. With Martha's marriage he would see his sister happily married, his wife gratified to be full mistress of her own home, the respect of his family increase, and his own honor raised in public opinion.

All would be well yet, he told himself. He trusted his wife's discretion.

Lazarus raised his cup to be filled and joined in toast to old Uncle Simon—the grandest man living! May he live long and continue to enjoy God's favor!

CHAPTER 9

"And if anyone causes one of these little ones who believe in me to sin, it would be better for him to be thrown into the sea with a large millstone tied around his neck."

MARK 9:42

The shouting had been the worst part. The raised voices . . . the insults hurled viciously. Martha stared around, her heart pounding. She knew some of these people—had known them since she was a toddler! There was the baker, the potter, the potter's cousin who was apprenticing. With them was the wife of the tanner, the carpenter's niece, and an old woman with no living relatives. She knew them by name, could recite their family histories and the gossip that surrounded their lives. All had come on business to Jerusalem. Martha knew them, but she didn't know them this way.

"Whore! Slut!"

"Prostitute! Stone her!"

They had formed a circle around the woman, closing in on her menacingly. Someone had already kicked filth from the street into her face, and she was coughing, rubbing at her eyes, ducking her head.

"No, please!" Martha shouted, but the mob drowned out her voice.

A boy had picked up a rock the size of his fist, and he was tossing it speculatively into the air and catching it. Martha snatched it from his hands and slapped him on the back of the head.

"Samuel, you are too young to do this!" she said sharply, and the boy blushed and sidled away from her. He hadn't expected to see a village woman in the center of Jerusalem.

But she couldn't take away every stone from a crowd. Only a handful knew her, and of that handful, only the younger children would listen to her. No, she couldn't play mother hen to all of them!

It had begun that morning. Mary had not met up with Martha

as she had promised to, near the Temple. Martha had worried herself sick. A villager like her did not trust a city, and now with her
sister hours late, the worst fears scuttled into her mind. But what
could she do? She tried to look for her. She circled away from the
Temple, hoping to catch a glimpse of her sister's familiar face. As she
wandered the streets she dared not call her name. What if someone
heard? The rumors were vicious enough as it was.

So she had searched and searched. And prayed. Oh, how she had
prayed! Begging God for her sister's safety. And then she had seen
her—only a glimpse, but it had been enough. Mary was on her
knees, barely covered by a tattered tunic, her white face upturned in
pleading to a small band of men with nothing but bloodlust in their
eyes. And Martha's stomach had dropped. It had finally happened.

"Caught in the act, you little whore!" a man snarled. "You will
die for this!"

"No!" Mary begged. "Please! Let me go!"

"Let you go?" the man laughed callously. "Oh, no, not this
time! You will face the circle, that's what you'll do!"

Her eyes were wide with terror, and her legs collapsed beneath
her, her body dropping to the ground. They dragged her on, her
legs scraping against the paving stones. Her hair was uncovered, and
her robe, which had been thrown hastily on, had pulled down at the
shoulder. Her mouth was agape, and, scrambling to her feet and
breaking free, she jerked herself backward, but to no avail.

"Please!" she shrieked. "Oh, please!"

Behind her Simon had stepped out of the house. Uncle Simon?
What was he doing in Jerusalem at the exact time they were there?
The two sisters had come to buy some fabric. A wedding was coming up, and they wanted new clothes for the festivities. Mary had insisted that they shop separately, wanting to get her sister a gift, she
claimed. It had seemed strange, but Martha reluctantly agreed. She
had guessed all along what Mary was going to do. Why hadn't she
stopped her? But her sister did this often now, and Martha's words
had fallen on deaf ears. They would meet at a certain time at a place
near the Temple. But why was Simon here? Why was he with
Mary? He was still wrapping his robe around his tunic, and he
looked at the scene with a lazy expression of amusement.

Martha had been about to call out to her uncle, but the words caught in her throat. Something was not right about this. Her uncle looked as if he was still dressing, but he was not leaving his own home. It was the house of someone unknown to her. Why would he be undressed in another man's house?

"I didn't do it!" Mary sobbed. "You are mistaken! I have done nothing!"

"Didn't do it?" The taunting voice was Uncle Simon's. "What did you not do, my girl? What did you not do for me oh so willingly?"

He let out a laugh that chilled Martha's blood.

It all came together in her mind in a single rush. He had slept with her—had blatantly and publicly slept with his niece! It wasn't in their own town, so perhaps the people of Jerusalem wouldn't place the family association. She knew that he would never be punished—only Mary. He would be frowned upon, perhaps, for having hired a prostitute, but it was Mary who would receive the brunt of the people's condemnation.

"It's all lies!" Mary gasped. "It's lies!" And then she crumpled into hysterical sobs.

Martha dodged into a small alley. She couldn't do anything now as a group of men she easily recognized as Pharisees dragged her sister away. The religious men, the powerful men, they had caught her. Heart pounding in her chest, Martha ducked low when one of the men turned his head in her direction. All they needed was an excuse to vent their fury on one more woman. Pharisees didn't like women. Women were wicked, they said. Flawed and evil.

Why not drag the sister to be stoned as well? One prostitute in the family could point to a family flaw. Perhaps they would blame Martha for sheltering Mary and protecting her. One more wicked woman . . .

Simon followed the men closely as they hurried Mary toward the Temple. Her screaming had drawn the other people's attention, and they rushed to the spot to hear the evidence against her.

"Caught in the very act!"

"Unclothed when we came in!"

"We saw it all! No doubt about what she was doing."

Why the Temple? Martha stayed at the edge of the crowd. If they went crazy, she needed a way of escape!

The Temple courtyard was busy, encircled by tall stone walls with engraving along the sides. Stalls sold doves in wooden crates and small goats crammed into stalls that were too small for them. The smell of manure was almost overpowering, and mixed with the shouts of the angry townspeople were the calls of the merchants, selling their wares, unwilling to relinquish their position, even for a stoning. People who had been milling around, looking for the best bargain for their sacrifice offering, suddenly rushed to the side, pulling away from the angry throng. Mothers grabbed the hands of their children and hauled them a safer distance away. Other people rushed closer, wanting a look at whatever infamous woman was about to receive her punishment. It would be a story later to tell in their own little town, how they themselves had seen the shameless face of the harlot. People would be spellbound around a dinner table, listening to the story of a woman's death.

"Stone her!" A woman's voice went up, and others quickly picked up the chant. Martha looked around in panic. That was when she discovered that their own villagers were here! Shopping, perhaps, or were their motives closer to those of her uncle? They were people who had known Mary since her birth. Women who had actually assisted in her birth!

"No!" Martha shouted at them. "Not this time! Show mercy!"

No one listened or showed any concern for mercy. Not today. Today was about punishment—retribution and blood.

A woman near the front threw a spattering of pebbles that bounced off of Mary's skin. Was that Aniah, the wife of the tanner? It looked like her, but from this angle Martha couldn't be sure. A man spat at Mary, and a child near his side jumped up and down, yelling wordlessly in his little piping voice. The shouts around her grew louder and seemed to crash over them in rhythmic waves. She'd seen it before . . . when she was only a child. Martha knew what would happen. Mary cringed in the center of the angry mob, trying to shield her face from the barrage of small stones.

"Teacher, what do you say to this?" one of the Pharisees shouted.

Teacher? Whom were they talking to? Was a rabbi teaching in the Temple this morning? Were they really looking for advice?

Martha's mind reeled. Later she would be surprised at the thoughts that had flashed through her mind at that moment. How would she tell Lazarus? How would they bear the additional shame of one of their womenfolk being stoned for adultery? The village would do nothing to make it easier for them. Martha would have to cook, regardless of her heartbreak. No women would come forward to help her shoulder the burden of household work while she mourned for her sister. The evening chores began to run through her head, and she started to sort through them mentally. She would also have Mary's work to do.

The methodical cataloging of chores somehow helped to calm her panic. Then she saw Him.

Jesus was the one teaching that day. He pulled His prayer shawl from off His head and walked toward them. His eyes were bright and intent. And just as suddenly as a flood of relief swept over her, making her feel almost faint, she realized something else—Jesus, a family friend, was witness to the family shame! He was seeing Mary nearly naked and about to be punished for prostitution and adultery. Martha had a sudden urge to throw herself bodily in front of Him so that He could not look at the sight. It was humiliation, not only for Mary, but for the entire family—their public shaming.

Martha's body refused to cooperate with her mind, however. Her body felt sluggish and foreign, as if she were in a dream or a high fever. Jesus looked around at them wordlessly.

"What do you say, Teacher?" another man called. "We caught her in the very act of adultery! There were witnesses! What should we do with her?"

"Stone her!" a woman demanded, and several others joined in.

"It is the law of Moses, is it not?" another voice, deep and familiar, questioned.

Martha turned her attention to Uncle Simon. He stood with his arms crossed over his chest and his chin raised proudly. The wind ruffled his beard, and his eyes flashed in defiant fury. Uncle Simon. She felt no emotion toward him. Nothing at all. Yes, she knew what he had done. She had known his sins from when she was only a small girl. He had trapped his own niece, had slept with her in order to have her stoned . . . but Martha still felt nothing. Only numbness.

Jesus didn't seem to answer. Instead He stooped down out of

sight. People strained to see what He was doing. A moment later He stood up and looked pointedly at someone in the front row. The man turned and slipped away, dragging his child with him. Jesus stooped again, and still Martha could not tell what He was doing. Too many bodies were in the way. Another man mumbled something and eased out of the crowd. One by one they left, until they began fleeing in groups, looking back apprehensively.

Finally there was room enough, and Martha saw Jesus squatting on the ground, tracing what appeared to be words on the dusty paving stones with His finger. Martha could not read. She knew what writing looked like, but it wasn't a woman's place to learn it. A woman's role involved caring for the family and listening to her husband tell her what the Torah or other writing said. She looked down in wonder at the lines and swirls that Jesus made.

Never looking up, Mary clung to the torn tunic that barely covered her, hunched as if still waiting for the blows to fall on her back. A stoning never started with the head. Her body trembled in sudden shivers that came in waves.

"Where are they?" Jesus asked softly.

Mary sat motionless.

"The people who were condemning you," He said, putting His arm around her shoulder and pulling her to her feet. "Where are they?"

Opening her eyes, Mary glanced around. Her gaze fell on Martha and lingered there for a moment. Then she turned to Jesus.

"Gone," she whispered.

"I don't condemn you either," He said to her. Removing His outer robe, He wrapped it around her shoulders. "Now, go home, Mary, and start a new life."

Wordlessly she nodded.

Martha's mind suddenly regained control of her body, and she rushed forward, putting her arms around Mary's shoulders and pulling her close. When she glanced into Jesus' face as she gathered up her sister, He gave her what seemed an understanding smile. But did He really understand? Did He know how hard this was for her? Could a man grasp the shame of a woman?

It was a long, long walk back to Bethany. And as Martha hurried her sister along, people stopped to stare.

Mary had lost her veil. Martha pulled Jesus' too-large robe over her sister's hair. It was too big, and quite heavy, but at least it covered her. They would have to make sure that they returned it quickly. A cloak was costly, and most men had only one. Did Jesus have another one?

"It will have to do," Martha said quietly.

"I'm sorry!" Mary whispered, tears welling up in her eyes. "I'm so sorry, Martha!"

Her sister had nothing to say as they resumed the walk home.

CHAPTER 10

" 'These men who were hired last worked only one hour,' they said, 'and you have made them equal to us who have borne the burden of the work and the heat of the day.' "

MATTHEW 20:12

Martha could tell as she formed the dough into loaves that something was wrong. The texture didn't feel right. But she had used the same recipe her mother had followed, one handed down from her own mother. Martha never deviated from it. She didn't experiment with different ingredients or with different ways of grinding the flour. Nor did she add more or less oil or water. As always, she had tested her yeast before beginning. She frowned in frustration.

"What is it?" Mary asked.

"This bread's not right."

"Are you sure?"

Mary stood holding a wooden spoon in her hand from stirring the stew. It dripped savory broth onto the floor. Her sister sighed.

"Yes, I'm sure." Regardless, she put the loaves onto the wooden paddle and eased them into the oven. Baking them would not waste a fire already lit and cooled to the proper heat. The coals would burn down with or without the bread.

As Mary turned back to the stew she stepped into the puddle of stew on the floor, then stared in perplexity at the slippery spot. She had never been skilled in the kitchen.

After wiping her hands irritably on a cloth, Martha used the back of one hand to push a stray hair away from her eyes.

"You look ready to cry," Mary said.

"I am." An awkward smile flickered across Martha's face.

"Why?" Mary asked, concerned. She let go of the spoon and approached her sister. As the spoon slipped beneath the bubbling surface of the stew behind Mary, Martha sighed again.

"Because of the bread," Martha admitted.

"Oh, a little flour wasted isn't the end of things," Mary observed with a shrug. "We are not poor, are we?"

"It isn't that." Martha waved her hand. "I don't expect you to understand."

"It might turn out after all," Mary said hopefully.

"It won't! It won't turn out! I know it won't!"

"Then make more tomorrow and stop worrying!" her sister replied with equal exasperation.

Martha shook head, then nodded toward the stew. "It needs to be stirred."

Mary returned to the bubbling pot. She looked into its depths, at her hands, then turned in a full circle, searching around herself. Martha felt a surge of satisfaction.

"The spoon is being cooked with the rest of it."

Mary let out a low laugh.

"A woman's world is nothing serious to you," Martha said irritably. "Obviously the bread is not the end of the world, but I did everything right. I measured. I followed the same recipe the women in our family have successfully used for generations. I tested the yeast. And still the bread failed."

"You have always done everything right," Mary said quietly. "And you feel as if you've failed?"

"Haven't I? I'm 27, unmarried, and living with my married brother. I can't even make bread properly! Where did I go wrong?"

"Maybe you didn't go wrong at all. You do have a marriage being arranged as we speak, don't you?"

"Even that is not the triumph a woman hopes for. I always felt I deserved more . . ."

"More than my fate," Mary said with a grimace.

"I didn't prostitute myself," her sister snapped. "I do deserve more!"

Neither spoke for several moments as Martha stared into the fire and Mary concentrated on the pot of stew.

"I need to know something," Martha said finally.

"Yes?"

"When Rachel mentioned Jebuseh, a look crossed your face."

"What kind of look?"

"That's what I'm asking you."

"It's pretty hard to remember one's own facial expressions," Mary replied.

"I need to know, sister." Martha's voice sounded tired. "Did you . . . know . . . Jebuseh before you reformed?"

"It was a long time ago," her sister said slowly.

"Did you?"

The women faced each other; their eyes locked. Martha stood with her arms crossed over her chest and her feet planted squarely. Mary let her hands hang limply at her sides. A pained expression filled her face.

"It is wrong to bring up old sins," Mary said at last.

"I must know!" Martha demanded, her voice rising. "I must know the truth so that I can face it like a woman and not have it come around and nip me from behind!"

"Yes. Yes, I did."

Martha let out a sigh. "How often?" she asked quietly.

"Only three or four times at most. Like most men, he desired me, but ended in resenting me and feeling repulsed by me because he blamed me for his sin."

"I see."

Thrusting the wooden paddle back into the hot recesses of the oven, Martha pulled out the now mangled and partially baked loaves. She dumped them in a basket beside the door and brushed her hands off.

Mary stood motionless, watching her.

"They were ruined anyhow," Martha said curtly. She passed her sister a new long-handled spoon. "Stir," she ordered.

Taking the spoon, Mary began to poke around in the stew, watching her sister warily. But Martha went out the doorway of the house and stared out in silence.

It was worse than she'd thought—even disgusting. She was going to marry a man who had bedded her prostitute sister. Did her sister's touch have to taint everything good in her life? Could nothing be left pure?

Martha hated her—hated everything Mary touched. She hated that men wanted her, and she hated that Mary would not stay away in another town where Martha didn't have to look at her. Was she doomed to her sister's fate?

Rachel didn't go into the kitchen. She left Martha and Mary alone. It made her uncomfortable to be with the two of them. They had a tense relationship, those two women, frightening and intimidating Rachel more than she cared to admit. Although she was the wife here, somehow she always gave in to her sisters-in-law. She didn't dare cross them. Even worse, Martha seemed different now that Mary had returned. The older sister was more irritable and secretive. If Rachel had been braver, she would have gone into that kitchen and reclaimed her domain. After all, it was her home. But she was not brave. Instead, she stayed in the common area, weaving at her loom. And even then it was not a case of being lazy. She was making clothing for her husband and was simply not cooking.

With a sigh Rachel leaned her head against her hand. It was strange how weak she felt. Could she be getting sick? Her stomach was heaving—it had been all morning. For the past few days it was as if she were waiting for a fever that never seemed to come. But the weakness . . . she felt as if she could sleep for a week straight!

And Rachel wasn't lazy. She prided herself on working hard and was determined to prove herself to her husband's family.

"Mistress?" the serving girl said. Rachel looked up at her, frowning at the expression of concern on the girl's face.

"What is it?"

"Do you need something? You don't look well."

"I'm fine." Rachel took another thread in her fingers and lifted one side of the loom, deftly inserting the thread before she pulled down the frame and pushed the thread firmly into place with the wooden shuttle. Just as quickly, she repeated the process.

Her stomach heaved again, and she paused in her work, willing the waves in her stomach to calm. She swallowed. Something rushed up her throat.

Rachel dashed to the front door in time to spill her breakfast onto the ground. For a few moments she bent over motionless, waiting to see if her stomach had finished emptying itself.

The girl mutely offered a clay cup of water. Rachel took it without looking at her and gingerly sipped.

"My mother has the same symptoms," the girl said, carefully looking toward the wall. Her voice was flat, as if she were talking to herself, or addressing the tall clay jar that her eyes rested on.

What was the girl saying? Rachel spat onto the ground, rinsing her mouth. Was she suggesting that Rachel was suffering with some beggar ailment?

"Babies cause it," the girl went on absently. "It's the first sign. Of course, my mother has had so many children, she recognizes it right away. Doesn't bother her much, she says."

Babies? Why hadn't she thought of it? Jerking upright, Rachel glanced toward the servant girl, then brushed past her, back into the house. Behind her, the girl was still making conversation with the pot.

"Sometimes some light tea can help with this time," she was saying. "And lying in a dark room."

A baby! The signs were all there. Why hadn't she considered the possibility? Her mother would have pinched her and called her a silly camel! Rachel's eyes misted at the thought of her mother. Her mother in the kitchen had been a welcome sight. She'd never felt locked out of the kitchen when she had lived at home with her parents. Suddenly she had the urge to sit down and cry.

Ask the advice of an older woman, one she could trust to keep her questions in confidence—that was the wise thing to do. Rachel must not appear ignorant of the ways of women. Her mother . . .

yes, she could visit her mother, who would offer her sympathy and understanding. But it was not her mother she was so desperate to impress. It was Lazarus' family. They must be the first to know that she was not barren—if she were indeed pregnant. This would be their child, born as their heir.

Uncle Simon. She paused, enjoying the luxury of her daydreams. Uncle Simon would be so happy. He would hug her and tell her that her child would be as beautiful as she was. And he would announce to the household that his nephew's wife had conceived!

That would be her day. A day belonging to Rachel alone, and she would look back on it for years to come. No one could steal her moment then. Not when she carried life in her womb.

It did not take long for her to wrap her veil over her head and head quickly out the door. Her aunt must be the woman to consult. Her aunt would be the one to tell Uncle.

"Stomach sick, you say?" Aunt Yardena asked, drying her hands on a cloth. "You must be nervous. Married life is harder than girls think."

"And very tired, too," Rachel added. "I'm not usually the nervous sort."

"Sick stomach and tired," Aunt Yardena mused, pursing her lips. "It could be . . ."

"Yes?" The older woman waited, watching Rachel with amusement.

"I could be pregnant, couldn't I?" The words came out of her in a rush. "Those are signs, aren't they?"

"They are signs." Yardena regarded her niece with a calculating eye. Rachel squirmed and looked down.

"I only wanted advice, that's all. I have never had a child. I wanted a woman's advice, someone who knows about these things."

"Advice I will give," Yardena said briskly. "You may very well be with child, but do not get too attached."

Rachel blinked.

"Don't speak of it until it is obvious to others," she warned. "You never know at this stage."

"My mother was strong in childbirth!"

"As was mine. I have lost four. Don't think about it too much. If something happens before people know, it's better that way. No need to explain anything. Your pain should be your own. Do not bother others with it."

"You think I might lose my child?" Rachel's voice quivered.

"You may, you may not. Time will tell. Women don't speak of lost babies. We simply go on to have more. It is better to be tough than to break each time you are disappointed."

"But what about Erda?"

"She is far enough along for it to be noticed. Erda has also proven herself strong in each pregnancy. She has not lost any children. Had she lost babies, I would not have spoken until she did."

Rachel stayed for only a few more minutes, murmuring small polite comments as Aunt Yardena looked at her with a strange calculating expression. As Rachel walked back to her own home her feet were heavy and her heart ached.

"O God of Abraham," she whispered. "I am with child . . ."

But for how long? Would she lose it? Would she be strong enough to carry this baby till the right time? Or would she be like so many other women, and lose as many babies as she birthed?

Uncle Simon. Sweet, kind Uncle Simon. He would be proud! If he were not ill right now, he would shout his joy and pronounce her blessed. He would give her a blessing to make her strong and healthy. And he would put his hand on her belly and tell her husband what a lucky man he was to have a wife like her.

Aunt Yardena would look a little disapproving. But then wives did not always approve of their husbands' exuberance. Wives preferred their husbands to be calm and reserved, like themselves.

But Uncle Simon would not be kept down! No, not even by his sickness. He would recover, she decided. After he got well he would tell her what a success she was, and how proud he was of her.

Might God bless Uncle Simon. Might He bring him back to full health, and give him many long years to watch this grandchild grow.

CHAPTER 11

*"Which is easier: to say to the paralytic, 'Your sins are forgiven,'
or to say, 'Get up, take your mat and walk'?"*

MARK 2:9

Martha pulled a twig out of her sister's unruly waves of hair, tugging harder at the thorny, brittle piece of wood than she needed to. It splintered into four pieces, one of which pricked Martha's finger. A small dot of blood appeared, and she put it into her mouth and sucked on it for a moment.

"You could have died," she said in a low tone.

Silence was the only reply.

"So selfish you are," she went on angrily. "Don't you think of me? I would have had to watch you stoned to death! Don't you think of me?"

More silence.

Abandoning her sister's hair, Martha took a wet cloth to her face, wiping the dust and tear streaks from her cheeks, and the mud formed from tears around her eyes. Mary was obedient, like a little child, shutting her eyes as her sister cleaned her face.

"I don't know why I keep protecting you. Any other family would have left you to your lot, you know."

Rinsing the cloth in a basin of water, Martha watched its contents turn muddy and dark. As she brought the cloth back to her sister's neck, Mary began to shake. At first it was a slight tremble, and then it wracked her entire body, her teeth chattering like someone with a fever.

"People here in Bethany will know," Martha snapped. "It's only a matter of time, and people will know!"

Mary wrapped her arms around her body, her hands shaking like leaves in the wind. She looked up at her sister, tears swelling in her eyes.

"I almost died!" she said suddenly, the words bursting out of her like the contents of a broken wineskin. "I almost died!"

"Almost," Martha said, shaking her head. "And news will travel, you mark my words!"

"They'd have killed me!" Mary insisted, her voice rising.

"Hush it," Martha replied coldly. "No use announcing it before time, is there?"

"I'd have died!" Hysteria filled the younger woman's voice.

"I said, Be quiet!"

Before she could even think, Martha raised her hand and slapped her sister solidly across the face. Mary blinked twice and shut her mouth, but her teeth continued to chatter and her breath came in short gasps. Her fingers clutched the heavy robe Jesus had given her, her broken nails biting into the fabric.

"Don't ruin His robe. We'll have to return it, and if you give it back with tears, it will look . . ."

Martha stopped. How would it look? Negligent? Disgraceful? What did it matter anymore? Jesus had witnessed the worst that He could see! He'd seen a whore about to be stoned! A damaged robe seemed so small compared to this. Only appearances. Nothing could be won back by appearances anymore.

Wash your face, their mother had said. And never leave your hair uncombed, because who knew if the wind would suddenly tear your veil from your head, exposing your hair to the world? If such a disgraceful thing happened, at least your hair would be combed and oiled.

Clean under the jars, their mother had said. Don't leave rings of unseen filth under the bottoms of pots. Who knew if someone might bump them, or push them aside for some unknown reason and expose the dirtiness? A kitchen was clean only if every corner and inch of it was clean.

Treat every man with respect, their mother had said. Give him reverence and honor. Who knew if he was not testing you for a family—testing your worth as a woman and a future wife? A woman's honor was gained over a lifetime and lost in a moment.

Because appearances mattered.

Their mother . . . Martha suddenly missed her desperately. Not that she wanted her to see their family's disgrace, but because she longed for her to say some words of wisdom that would bring everything into perspective. Perhaps she would say, "Gathered stones don't make a house," or "After the rain, the weeds sprout up, but after two days of sun, they wither again."

But this weed would not wither. The villagers would carefully water it. It would be spoken of as far as Jerusalem and would flourish. The village women would give this weed better care than a newborn baby. Because if Martha knew anything, it was that a village never forgot.

"I know what happened," she said after a few minutes. "I know it was Uncle."

Mary sucked in her breath, her cheeks going even more white than they had been, and Martha wondered suddenly if her sister were about to faint. The thought annoyed her. Mary had no right to be weak! She had no right to need her sister! Martha had done enough today, and she did not need to be picking Mary up off the ground.

But Mary did not faint.

"Yes," she said simply.

It was not so simple, this situation with their uncle. Martha knew what he had done to her sister for years now . . . what she had never been able to stop.

"Why did he turn you in to the authorities?" Martha asked, suddenly feeling very weak. "Why did he expose both of you that way?"

"Because he hates me. And other reasons, of course."

"What reasons? To hate you, I can understand. Men hate those who cause them to feel guilt."

Mary flinched. "I understand his hatred, too. But it was not about me, Martha. Nothing has ever been about me. I am not important. Uncle could have ruined me easily enough with some other man in the village. He didn't need to do this himself. They wanted to kill Him."

"Who?"

Martha hated this strange, clipped way Mary had of speaking. She spoke like a child, spilling out words that had significance to her, but not bothering to explain so another person could understand.

"Jesus, of course." Mary gave her an exasperated look. "Don't you listen to any gossip at all? The Pharisees hate Him! Jesus speaks against them. He calls them snakes and denounces their pompous ways."

"Uncle Simon hates Jesus?" Martha asked in disbelief.

"His influential friends hate Jesus," Mary said with a shrug. "It amounts to the same thing. Our esteemed uncle will pander after anyone richer or more powerful than he is."

"Jesus healed him." Martha instantly realized that she had only stated the obvious.

"And I am his responsibility, like a daughter." Mary's eyes were wide and innocent. "Yet he orders me to do things—things that go against all natural behavior between family members."

Yes, yes, Martha knew that. "I pray to God that he dies," she whispered.

"You are not a wife yet."

"Maybe God will listen anyway. I pray to God that his leprosy will come back and eat him away, starting with his rotten heart."

"I don't."

"Why not?"

"Because in my own way I'm just as wicked as he is," Mary said, raising her eyes to meet her sister's gaze. Her eyes were bright and fervent. "And today I was forgiven!"

Jacob leaned back against a pillow and interlaced his fingers behind his head. His mind was not on the meal he had just eaten, and he didn't see his wife taking the clay plates away and removing dishes into the kitchen. He ignored the nattering questions of his youngest boy, and absently freed his beard from the boy's curious grip. Now nearly 8 years old, his oldest son lounged not far from his father, imitating his father's posture and position. The boy's sister, 4 years old, followed after her mother, chattering away about a mouse she had seen, or something like that.

It was the life of a family man, soon to be the life of a patriarch. Much more responsibility was falling on his shoulders. He already felt the burden of providing for his wife and children. Erda was a good wife—thrifty and moderate in her ways. She was a strong support for a man, but he still felt his duty toward her, to keep her in good standing in the village. Thus she must have ample money at her disposal, not only for preparing for dinners and entertaining, but also for her personal use. Her high-quality clothing and expertly woven sandals spoke of their status as well. The woman's taste was impeccable, and quite expensive.

As for his children, they would grow up before he knew it. His boys would require homes of their own and would need to find wives. His daughter would have to be kept in proper condition to be marriageable. And what if she weren't? She seemed pretty enough now, as a small child, but what if she grew up to be more like Martha? Family resemblances did follow sometimes. What if little Dinah turned out to be just like her father's cousin—plain?

The thought disconcerted him, and he did not want to think of it. Martha had always been a little different. She'd always been so earnest . . . so intense. While she hadn't been exactly bad looking, she lacked any kind of spark or glow that attracted a man to her. As she grew up, any blush of prettiness that she might have had had seemed to flee. At least that was how he felt about her. He had recognized that she had been a possible bride for him, since she was his cousin and the right age. Because she had seemed to know this as well, he remembered her watching him with a doe-eyed expression. It had been embarrassing for him, especially since she had not even bothered to hide it. While she had been too young to maintain a womanly reserve, it had still made him shy around her, and therefore unduly gruff.

"Martha, go pretend to cook something," he'd tell her, and her eyes would well up with tears.

"I cook," she'd say defensively. "I don't pretend. I can do all the work alone!"

"Then go do it," he would say pointedly. "Stop bothering me."

As she got older, she did acquire more womanly reserve, hiding her feelings more. Even though she still watched him, she kept her expression veiled. Did she still long for him? He was no longer sure. But she watched him. It made him uncomfortable, her constant observation.

Other young men noticed her, though, and seemed to see something he didn't. Sometimes he felt jealous noticing them eye her. Once he'd kicked the crippled beggar . . . Karlan the Cripple, who was about the same age as Jacob. Karlan had watched her as she passed by with a group of girls her own age, and Jacob had seen something in his expression that disgusted him. Cripples weren't meant to look at women that way! They should beg and keep their eyes focused on the dirt! And so he had kicked him as he passed by. Defending the honor of the family, he told himself. When Karlan let out a puff of breath and grunted, Jacob felt satisfied. He would have felt more satisfied if the beggar had cried out, but the stubborn cripple refused to make a sound. At least he'd lowered his eyes back to the dirt.

But when Jacob had looked away from Crippled Karlan, he had seen Martha's eyes on him. And this time something else crept into her expression: surprise and disapproval. It seemed that she did not like him kicking beggars. Well, she wasn't a man. She didn't know what lurked behind the watchful eyes of other men. But he did. And she'd just have to trust the men of her family to do what was right by her.

Mary was different, though. Playful and fearless, she didn't seem to care if Jacob lived or died. And when Mary became known—when her promiscuity provided a topic of common village talk—he had wanted what she gave other men. He felt comfortable around her. But still Martha watched him.

Embarrassingly enough, Mary wouldn't pay any attention to him. She seemed to think him below her somehow, and his father had watched the silent exchanges with growing anger.

"Leave her alone!" he'd snap. "What kind of filthy boy are you?"

Yes, his moral and upright father. He'd always been moral and upright. The Pharisees always were. Simon was so correct in all his ways and religious observances that Jacob had felt himself hating his father. Was the man not human at all?

But she was his cousin . . . not a girl to be dallied with. Her reputation might already be tarnished, but he should not take part in the tarnishing—no matter how much he wanted to. The fact was, however, that she would not let him near her.

"Jacob, you are such a stick," Mary used to say. "I don't understand you at all, nor do I care to."

And she had meant those words—he was sure of it. He could still see her, her veil slipping teasingly back to expose her hair and her lips pouting pettishly as she talked. To her, he was a stick—uninteresting and dull. It only made him crave her all the more. Not for a wife, of course, because his father would choose one for him.

No, he wanted her the way every other man did. He wanted a turn.

Now, as a married adult man with a houseful of children of his own, he still longed for his turn. Somehow he felt left out. Supposedly she had reformed. "Reformed"—that was the word she used, wasn't it? Now that she was reformed, he didn't know if he was still a stick to her or not.

And perhaps even worse, Martha still watched him. He hated those observant eyes—the way she absorbed every scrap of detail and organized it neatly in her too-intelligent mind. She needed to be diverted by her own husband and children. But she had none.

His father's orders came to his mind. It was true—his wife had confirmed the rumor. Martha was about to be betrothed. Lazarus was finalizing the details. She would soon be busy with her own life instead of putting her old-maid attention into everyone else's. At least that was Lazarus' plan. Jacob's father had another one.

The night was cool, and Jacob could feel the tips of his toes beginning to feel cold. His wife was bustling the children to bed, and he looked with appreciation at her as she bent over the youngest boy and gathered him up into her arms. Erda had discarded her outer robe, and she stood in her tunic, the light from the oil lamps that stood on small shelves and niches illuminating her form through the fabric. The off-white of her tunic contrasted with the crimson and brown tapestries hanging from the walls, and she carefully sidestepped a plate of raisins lying on the floor near the boy. She stood flat footed, with her legs straight as she bent to pick up their son, and he was still amazed at her flexibility. Her hair was glossy and straight, and her arms were well muscled. A handsome woman, she was sturdy and rounded, solid and comforting. His father had chosen well for him. While she was no Mary, in a way that was something to be thankful for. A prostitute was nothing to be coveted.

He could not help feeling a pang of guilt at what he had done to Martha. True, they were his father's orders, but he would carry them out. It was cruel, and he knew it. If Erda discovered it, would her easy, affectionate attitude toward him change? Would she stiffen, seeing Old Simon's cruelty in her husband? His father had always been the same—righteous and unyielding. Such holiness had the force of a hammer. But this . . . this last order he had given his son. It did not have the mask of righteousness. It was something altogether different.

"The children are in bed," Erda said softly, and Jacob roused himself from his thoughts. He forced a smile.

"You are a good woman."

She stood looking down at him, seeming undecided as whether to go to bed herself, or to stay with him. Finally she sank down to the ground next to him, careful not to touch him. Pulling her legs up against her, she wrapped her arms around them. She was taking a chance, but he would not send her away. Somehow he needed some comfort this night.

"Would you like something to eat?" she asked finally.

"Food will not help me tonight," he said, shaking his head.

"What will help?"

"I don't know. I've done something I regret."

"Will you tell me?" she asked quietly.

"No."

She wouldn't push him. He knew that. A good wife, she knew her place. After a few minutes she got up and quietly went out, leaving him alone with his thoughts.

Was it really so cruel? Perhaps he was only hurrying along something that would have happened eventually anyway. Perhaps it would not be painful after all.

But he knew he was wrong. It would undoubtedly be painful. And he would have caused it.

CHAPTER 12

"But even the dogs under the table eat the children's crumbs."

MARK 7:28

Waiting seemed to be the lot of a woman's life. A woman waited to be noticed . . . to be allowed to speak . . . for a man to marry her . . . for children. She could not simply go out and make anything happen. That was the realm of men. Men caused the world to function as it did. Women waited for the men to work on their behalf.

I wish I never had to wait again, Martha thought to herself. *I wish I could go out like a man and secure my own future!*

It was a bad thought, wasn't it? She was really wishing to be a man. While it was wrong to wish that you belonged to a different station in life, it was worse still to wish to be a part of a different gender! One must be content with one's place in life. It will never change. Born into it, you would stay there, more or less. If you were a man, you would live in the home of your father. As a younger son, you would live in a home your father helped prepare for you. And if you were a woman, you lived in the home of your husband, and your husband would be, most likely, the same station as your father. Things really did not change much.

"You are going to beat that dough into a brick!" Rachel said with a laugh.

Pulling herself out of her reverie, Martha smiled self-consciously. She could feel the dough already binding into a tough mass, and she put it down onto the low table and gave it a pat.

"It might be a brick already," she confessed. "I'm sorry—my mind is not in my work."

The oven was nicely heated, the coals having cooled from glowing red to a somber black, but still hot enough to bake the loaves. Rachel would turn the flatbread by quickly pinching one edge of the loaf and flipping it over, using her other fingers to support the large piece so that it did not tear or fall apart during the process. The cooked side of the bread was bubbly and browned to perfection. When the bread was done on the underside, Rachel snatched it off the coals as fast as a hopping grasshopper and plopped it onto a growing pile.

"A wedding is a happy time," Rachel nattered. "The feast will be wonderful! The whole village will be there to celebrate, and all the women of the family will come to cook . . . Erda . . . Shiloh . . . Tisha . . . Aunt Yardena . . . It will be such fun to work together for a happy time."

Mary glanced toward her sister, then looked back down to her own work.

"This time for Uncle Simon's household is one of sadness," she said quietly after a few moments. "Especially for you, Rachel."

"It is," Rachel replied.

"You would rather celebrate a wedding than wait for a death."

"We are not waiting for a death! Do not say that sort of thing. Tell her, Martha."

"He is dying, Rachel. It is better to be prepared so that you do not fall apart when the inevitable happens. You are a married woman. No childish carrying on for you. The men will wail and lament. They can lie on their mats all day if they so choose. You are a woman, and while you might cry, you will then get up and make the food to serve to the men. A woman does not have the luxury of giving into grief. Grieve if you must, but grieve when you have time!"

Rachel gave an exasperated huff in the direction of both her sisters-in-law. Martha shut her mouth, refusing to give the young woman the lecture she deserved. Now was not a time for lectures, in spite of Rachel's obvious need of one. She behaved as almost a girl. So spoiled. Not having toughened up yet, she was, in a way, still playing house. While going through the motions of keeping her own home, she hadn't developed the calluses yet. It would seem that when Uncle Simon finally died, it would fall to Martha, as usual, to care for the household. Rachel would be entirely helpless, like the men, and Mary, ironically, would be of more use than their brother's wife.

"For my wedding," Rachel began a well-known theme, "all the women of the family cooked for days for the feast! Lazarus came late one night to take me to his house, and the minute I was gone, even though it was terribly late, the women began to cook. I believe it helped them to feel better. I was the favorite, you know."

Rachel glanced up from her work and gave Martha a look of childish wisdom.

"It is always hard when a girl is taken by her husband," Martha said, nodding.

"I think it must have been harder on my mother. She loved me so much, and what would she do without me in the house?"

"The same we'll do in the house without Martha, I assume," Mary put in with a chuckle.

Rachel cast Mary a look of unveiled disapproval. She did not like the use of "we" to link herself and Mary in any way at all, Martha knew.

What would they do without me in the house? Martha wondered. Rachel did not know how spoiled she was. Although she left much of the work to Martha, Martha hadn't minded apart from some head shaking and tongue clucking. She liked keeping busy. It kept her mind on the familiar paths of domestic chores, instead of wandering about in the past or the fantasized future.

But she would have a wedding! It made her almost giddy inside. A wedding. A bridegroom would come to fetch her late one night, and she would be carried off like a young girl, balanced on the back of a donkey and led away from her home by her new husband's male relatives, laughing and celebrating the joy of a marriage. It was comic, almost. A woman of her age being taken off like a young thing crying for her mother. Well, Martha would not be homesick for her mother. And she would not be wide-eyed and terrified. She would know what to expect . . . for the most part. The work would be familiar. Only the house would be different. And the drastic change of suddenly having a husband to deal with instead of a brother. But even the husbandly demands would not be too burdensome, she decided, since there would be a first wife to curb the old man through her jealousy.

And there *would* be jealousy. How would she deal with this new domestic situation? Would she look up to the first wife as a mother? Would she be obedient to her, or would she push to gain her own power in the household?

Once she was pregnant, her position would be more definite . . . once she was pregnant . . . A sudden fear gripped her that she would be barren . . . her womb closed by God for some unknown reason. Or would the reason really be so unknown? Martha would know the reason. She would know what her punishment was for.

"What could be taking so long?" Mary asked suddenly, wiping her hands on a cloth and pushing absentmindedly at her hair, leaving a floury streak through its waves.

Martha was silent.

"Really," her sister pressed, "this should not be taking so long, should it?"

"Have you ever made these arrangements?" Martha asked her coolly. "I imagine it takes some time. It is a financial discussion, after all."

"Maybe so." Shaking her head, Mary turned back to her work.

The wind outside was picking up, driving dust and grit against the sides of the house. Through the tiny window just below the ceiling Martha could see the billows of dust blowing through the air, and she dropped the heavy leather flap that would block it from getting into the food. It was not a perfect covering, and grit still drifted inside, but it was better than nothing. She spat some dirt from her mouth that ground irritatingly between her teeth.

For years and years, generations even, the dirt had blasted against the sides of their house. All the houses looked the same from the outside, whether the inhabitants were wealthy or poor. The size of the building might betray social scale, or even the part of the village itself, but a stranger to the village would have no other hint. It was the inside of a house that told.

And the inside of this house held countless memories for Martha. The plastered walls of the living area and the carefully painted borders of the room . . . The tapestries that had hung as long as she could remember, except for one or two that Rachel had changed . . . The same upper sleeping quarters that Martha had slept in as a small girl . . . The kitchen arranged in much the same way as Martha's own mother had had it . . . The spices hung to dry in the same place away from the window to avoid moisture from the rain, but also away from the fire to avoid letting the heat destroy the fragrance and taste . . . She looked around the kitchen lovingly. Would her own child regard her new kitchen in her married home the same way she did this one? And would her own sons and daughters think fondly back on their mother's ways of doing things?

But no, the kitchen would not be hers, would it? It would belong to the first wife. It would be the touch of the first wife that made that home. Yet the children would be Martha's!

The front door slammed, and all three women suddenly popped

their heads up to listen for Lazarus' approach. If he had brought a guest, dashing out with their heads uncovered would be a social travesty. Instead, they waited, frozen in the safe female domain of the kitchen area, their veils flung back, their hands motionless, and their ears pricked.

Lazarus let the door bang shut behind him, listening to the clatter that did nothing to relieve his frustration. He would have banged it again if he weren't convinced that the neighbors would notice. The dust in the air tickled his nose and made his skin itch. His robe caught on the clinging grass of a broom left against the wall, and it irritated him further. Although the urge to kick the broom swept over him, he refrained. Glancing toward the kitchen area, he saw three wide-eyed faces staring at him through the doorway. It was strange how grown women could look so much like girls at a time like this!

"Good evening, brother."

It was Mary. Leave it to her to be the first to address him. Martha and Rachel would be holding back, not wanting to infringe on him . . . waiting . . . waiting for him to feel comfortable enough to share his news, allowing him, as the man, to initiate the contact. Mary, on the other hand, failed to see the point. Ordinarily he would be annoyed with her for her lack of discretion, but not today. Today he was relieved to face his obstinate sister.

"Sit," she ordered. "Eat something. Have some goat milk."

Lazarus complied and took the frothy cup of milk offered to him. Rachel vanished to fetch his meal, and Martha watched him, her expression veiled. Finally, she turned and disappeared into the courtyard.

He didn't want to share any news. Not today. If he could only wait—wait until he had good news. The bearer of happy tidings instead of . . . What was he now? A failure. A man who failed to provide for his sister.

Mary had seemed to sense the reality of the situation quite quickly. She gave him an understanding glance and turned her attention away from him.

It wasn't entirely his fault, though! No, he may have failed, but it wasn't because of total incapability. Jebuseh had been so close . . . he'd been truly interested in Martha—had looked past her plain looks and seen the valuable woman she was. And then something changed. Lazarus couldn't be sure what exactly, but the man who was willing to negotiate had suddenly closed up and become evasive.

"Let us finalize our new relationship," Lazarus had said.

"There are still details to discuss," Jebuseh had replied.

"Details, of course . . ." Lazarus had not wanted to seem rude.

"So we will come to an agreement at another time, my friend. Put the matter aside. Come drink with me."

"Such details could be addressed at this time," Lazarus had pressed. "I'm sure we can come to a satisfactory settlement for all involved."

"A man must think. I have another wife to consider, of course. I must not be rash in my judgment."

"Martha is a sweet woman," Lazarus persisted. "She is eager to please, works hard, and never wastes any time in idle talk or gossip. She is admirable in every way! Your wife will have a much easier life because of your choice to marry Martha. Martha will run the house expertly and will endeavor to please your beautiful wife in all that she does—"

"I do not doubt that," Jebuseh interrupted, waving his hand dismissively. "I have seen her virtues."

"Then, come, let us make an agreement."

"Another day, my friend." Jebuseh's voice was firm. Lazarus had no choice but to drop the subject and discuss the rising price of wheat for as long as he could pretend to be comfortably chatting with a friend. Then he had excused himself—too early, he feared now—and left for home.

Perhaps he should have stayed longer, just to prove that marrying off his sister was not his primary reason for the visit. Had he shown too much desperation? The man did not want to take a woman who was forced onto his hand. Stupid! Why had he allowed himself to react so quickly?

"It's your favorite," Rachel said softly, placing the hot plate of food onto the floor beside him. He could smell the heady scent of cumin and garlic, and he tore a piece of fresh bread, still soft and warm. It was a delicious meal, he could see, but his heart was not in it as he chewed slowly, not even tasting the cucumbers pickled with fresh mint.

Martha had come to refill his cup of goat milk, and she sat down a few feet away and watched him thoughtfully. Her expression was guarded, and he wondered what was passing through her mind. He pitied her. This would not be an easy time for her—waiting to see if a man would marry her or not. As a man he could not even imagine her discomfiture, but he could not see it, either. She hid her feelings well. His sister was an admirable woman.

But he needed to tell her something, however. This torturous waiting game could not go on all night.

"I spoke with Jebuseh today." He swallowed his mouthful of food with difficulty. His meal felt like rocks in his belly.

"Oh?" She gave him a quick, careful glance out the corner of her eye.

"The process is long," he said slowly. "Negotiations are still taking place."

"I see." Some of the tension left her mouth.

"There seems to be some sort of . . ." He paused, shaking his head. "I don't know exactly. A hitch, of some sort."

"A hitch?"

Why did she keep answering with two words? And the same tone their mother had used when she had been angry, but unable to show it in front of their father.

"Jebuseh won't commit yet," Lazarus confessed. "I pressed him, but to no avail. Perhaps that was a mistake."

Martha nodded. He was waiting for her to tell him that it was all right and that the marriage itself might not have been ideal. But she simply accepted his words, and offered no forgiveness or comfort for his failure. It was his alone to bear.

Lazarus looked up at his wife, who stood staring toward the kitchen with a tight expression around her mouth. She was chewing the inside of her cheek, and for just a moment, he saw true anger pass over her face. But it instantly vanished, and she did not look at him.

"Rachel."

She turned slowly. "I hope you enjoy your meal, husband," she said formally.

He sighed. Yes, she was angry—and had every reason to be. She had been very close to being mistress of her own home, and now, if Lazarus could not fix whatever blunder that had caused Jebuseh to retract, she would never truly be mistress.

A much stronger woman than Rachel was, Martha intimidated her. His sister was also much more difficult to marry off. She was . . . difficult. Lazarus pushed his plate away. He may have been the man of this house, but he was also outnumbered. The thought suddenly flashed through his mind that he wanted a son. He needed another male in this house. On days like this, three strong-willed women seemed to be too much to contend with.

CHAPTER 13

"And I declared that the dead, who had already died, are happier than the living."

ECCLESIATES 4:2

Martha had to accept the situation. She had no choice but to wait again. Perhaps God would soften the heart of Jebuseh, and he would make the betrothal final. Or perhaps Lazarus was simply being too sensitive, as men could be, and his fears were unfounded. But she had no way to find out anything for herself. Her betrothal was being arranged in the world of men, and it did not concern her yet. It would involve her only after the men had struck a deal and the finalities were legally binding.

Lazarus . . . she knew this was hard on him. Her brother had always said that he believed that Jesus had raised him from the dead because he had not finished his duty on earth. His sisters were his responsibility, and he would not leave them to face the world without the protection of a husband. He would provide for them, he promised. And when Lazarus promised something, he could be counted on. No one took his responsibilities more seriously.

But no matter how solid a man's character, no matter how reliable and good he is, there are forces stronger than he. And one day Lazarus had died. Tears came to her eyes even now as she thought about it.

⁓

"Have you heard yet?" Martha asked anxiously. "Did He send word?"

The laborer shook his head. With a sigh she turned away. It wasn't the man's fault. He was here helping out since Lazarus had fallen ill. She should be grateful to him for his kindness, not irritated that he could not give her the news she wanted.

"Mary, send the girl for more water!" Martha called as she swept back into the house. "And when she's done, there is bedding we must wash out."

If she could control her surroundings, perhaps the worst would not happen. Or if she could be organized enough, perhaps she could fight off the future.

As she approached the room in which her brother lay she slowed her pace. His fever was high, and no matter how much cool water she sponged over his head, and no matter how she fanned him, his body only seemed to grow hotter. He was in a delirium and would say strange things.

"The locusts are coming," he murmured, tossing in discomfort. "There are too many . . ."

Martha sank to her knees next to him and pulled the cloth from his head. It was already sickeningly warm. Brushing his moist hair off his forehead, she looked down onto her brother's ashen face.

"I sent word for Jesus to come," she said softly. "Don't worry. He'll be here! If He will heal lepers, He'll heal His close friend. Just hold on, my brother. It will be all right."

The fact that Jesus had not sent word yet worried her. It had been two days since she had dispatched the request, and the messenger had returned. What could be more important just now? What could be keeping Him? She hated to admit it, but she was beginning to wonder if Jesus would come at all.

Lazarus let out a deep sigh and opened his eyes. She smiled down at him, trying to look as reassuring as possible.

"I'm tired," he said in a faint voice.

"Don't worry," she replied quietly. "Just rest."

"Where is my mother?"

His mind had wandered back to his childhood, she realized sadly. He was remembering being a boy. But his boyhood had not lasted as long as it should have. Their parents had died too soon, leaving him with too many responsibilities.

"She's not here right now. But I am."

What had their mother done for them when they were sick? She used to hold their heads on her lap and stroke their hair while she talked to them. It was comforting. How long had it been since her little brother had been comforted?

Gently Martha lifted Lazarus' head and put it onto her lap. She stroked his hair away from his face and began to hum. He looked up into her face, his eyes fixed on hers in a sort of bewildered expression.

"Everything will be all right, brother. You are sick now, but the messenger said he overheard Jesus say that your illness would not end in death. You will be all right. Fevers pass."

He didn't answer her.

Lazarus. Poor, dear Lazarus. He'd always taken his responsibilities toward the family so seriously. Had always wanted to please, always wanted everyone else to be satisfied and happy. And he always saw the best in people, even if the worst was glaringly obvious. It was his most frustrating trait, but if that was the worst one could say about a man, he had done well in life.

But he wasn't just any man. He was her little brother. The one who worked so hard to provide for them . . . who did his best to keep their reputation strong in the community so that one day soon he could arrange a good marriage for her . . . the one who had grown up with her and seen her at both her worst and her best and loved her all the same. This was her brother, whom she'd seen develop from a toddling baby into a spunky child. She'd watched him slide into the moody years of his early teens, watched him discover his appreciation of the village girls, and watched him shaken under the grief of their parents' death. Throughout the years he'd teased her, annoyed her, protected her, and stood by her. He was her brother.

And in life, who was closer than your brother? Raised by the same people, he understood your family—understood you. He shared your complaints and could communicate with you using a single look. Even after a woman got married, her closest relationship was with her brothers or sisters. A husband was for honor. He was for children. But a brother was for life.

And now her brother lay in her lap like a little child, staring up at her with that strange bewildered expression.

"How do you feel?" she asked him softly.

Again no answer.

"Lazarus? How do you feel now?"

Still no response. When she looked closer, her heart pounding like thunder in her chest, she saw that his eyes had gotten glassy, and while they were still looking upward toward her, they weren't focused on anything at all. He was still. So very still.

And that was when her tears began to flow. Because she knew what had happened. Her little brother, the boy who was always too earnest and trusting . . . the man who took his responsibilities so seriously . . . the brother who had been her only support . . . was dead in her lap.

Martha let her head drop forward, and the tears came silently, chokingly. They filled her until she thought that she would drown in them, and they spilled out of her with slow heaves.

Jesus had said He'd come. Jesus had said Lazarus would not die. Jesus had lied.

The extended family helped make the funeral arrangements. Although always the strong one, Martha could not handle everything alone. She and Mary washed Lazarus' body and covered him in herbs and oil to fight off the smell of death. They looked down on his face that now looked so unlike him before wrapping him in strips of linen. It was the last thing they could do for him, and they did it with care.

There would be no more meals prepared for him. No more lentils and broad beans cooked because he loved them. No more joking in the evenings or long talks on Sabbath afternoon. But there was this—the preparation for burial.

As the days passed, Martha began to feel angrier and angrier. She had sent word—had told Jesus that His friend was ill! Jesus should have come! He should have, but He didn't! Lazarus didn't have to die. He could still be with them. Now the women were dependent on their next-closest male kin: Uncle Simon. It was a loathsome thought. The very man who had ruined them would now be their only protector in society. But it didn't have to be this way. It could have been different, if Jesus had only said one word . . . if Jesus had only said "Be healed" from even miles away. But He hadn't.

Lazarus had been dead four days before Jesus arrived. He came with His friends, traveling on foot, and when He appeared just outside the village, Martha was there to meet Him. What else could she do? Where else could she turn? The first thing to come out of her mouth was "If You'd come earlier, Lazarus would still be alive!"

It was reproachful, and she meant every word.

"Don't you believe?" He asked her gently.

Jesus stood there, His dark eyes focused on hers, and the warm late-afternoon wind rustling His hair, already dusty from His journey. His clothes were equally dusty, and He looked tired, but He would not break His gaze from hers.

"I believe that whatever You ask God will give You," she said. But He hadn't asked. And now Lazarus was dead.

"Your brother will rise again," Jesus said.

"At the resurrection," she said quietly. "And until then, I shall miss him."

Tears welled in her eyes, and she fought them back. Her throat was tight, and she took a deep, wavering breath, trying to control her emotions.

"I am the resurrection."

Martha was silent, looking at Him, watching the fabric of His cloak flapping in the wind that was beginning to pick up.

"I am the life. If a man believes in who I am, he will live even though he dies."

She blinked at him. What was He saying?

"Whoever lives and believes in who I am will never die. Do you believe this?"

"Yes, Lord. I know that You are the Messiah, the Son of God."

"Where is your sister?"

"At home. Many have come to give their condolences . . . Someone had to stay."

"Will you go get her?" He asked.

Something in His gentle, respectful voice made Martha want to lean on Him and cry out her grief, but she could not. A woman must stand up under her grief—must always go on. She does not have the luxury that a man has of venting sorrow. Things must still be done. The living still needed attending to.

When Martha returned with her sister, she watched Mary throw herself at Jesus' feet, dissolving into tears. Her lips in a thin, disapproving line, Martha stared at her. This was so like Mary! Always venting her emotions like a man . . . always acting so inappropriately. Mary, her face against the feet of Jesus, sobbed out the same words that Martha had used.

"If You had been here, Lazarus would not have died!"

She was an embarrassment always. Even in the presence of death, Mary could not be discreet or proper. In everything she lost all sense of decorum. It was disgusting, and Martha's old feelings of disapproval and disgust rose up in her again.

"Where have you laid him?" Jesus asked.

"We'll show You," Mary said, rising to her feet.

And then Jesus looked past her and directly into Martha's eyes. She felt as if He saw her . . . truly saw her. The pain inside of her that she could not release. Her disappointments and hopes, all dashed now with the death of her brother. And as Martha stood fighting back her tears, Jesus' eyes filled with sorrow, misted with tears that spilled down His cheeks.

It was as though He was crying for her—releasing all the pain that she could not—and she held His gaze, sharing the pain.

"See?" people began to murmur, "He loved him!"

But it was more than that. Jesus loved her, too . . .

People had followed to the tomb. Martha imagined that they sought to offer support. But why did Jesus come here? Was it as hard for Him to believe as it was for her? Did He need to see the tomb itself in order to accept the loss of His friend?

The tomb had been carved into the side of the mountain. A large stone had been rolled in front of the entrance, and mortar had been packed into the crevices. It was better to seal up the decay, or it would smell . . .

"Roll away the stone," Jesus ordered.

Martha's breath caught in her throat. Murmured disapproval came from many, and she sighed. Must Jesus see His dead friend before He could accept the loss? But it was so late—the time for viewing the body was over. Now it was time to let it rest.

"Lord," she whispered. "It's been four days. Lazarus . . . he . . . has started to smell now . . ."

"Roll it away," Jesus repeated. "Didn't I tell you to believe in who I am?"

The people glanced at her, wondering what she would do. But what could she? It was her place to say what could be done with her brother's body, but to refuse Jesus? If He needed to see the body, she would not stop Him. She nodded to several young men, and they began to unseal the tomb. As they hammered away at the mortar, the foul smell seeped out. Women pulled up their veils, and men covered their noses and mouths.

Wondering if He was satisfied, Martha looked up at Jesus, but He didn't seem to notice the stench at all. He was staring at the tomb with absolute attention.

"Lazarus!" He suddenly called.

A few titters rippled through the crowd. Had the sun touched Him? Lazarus was dead!

"Lazarus!" Jesus repeated, His voice filled with authority. "Come out here!"

Martha held her breath, unsure of what she was waiting for . . . but she heard rustling in the tomb, and she wondered suddenly if a wild animal had scuttled inside.

And before she knew it, she saw the whiteness of the cloths she had wrapped around her brother so carefully. And there he was, on his hands and knees, at the entrance of the tomb, struggling with the cloths, his face still covered.

"Unwrap him!" Jesus directed. "Lazarus, how are you, My friend?"

The rest of what happened was a blur for Martha. Later she re-

membered her heart pounding and her knees going weak. Babbling
her thanks to Jesus, she rushed forward to help tear the cloths from
Lazarus' body. The cloths stank horribly, but underneath them
Lazarus was whole and well again. He blinked in the sunlight and
accepted another man's robe to wrap around his shoulders.

And as everyone went back to Lazarus' house to celebrate the
unbelievable miracle, Martha followed behind, trying to grasp what
had happened. Jesus fell back from the crowd around Lazarus.

"Lord . . ." Martha said, unsure of how to continue.

"Martha, even while you were crying, holding your brother on
your lap, I was thinking of you," He gently told her.

"Come eat with us!"

It was all that Martha knew how to give.

CHAPTER 14

*"Again, I tell you, it is easier for a camel to go through the eye of
a needle than for a rich man to enter the kingdom of God."*

MATTHEW 19:24

The fever seemed to be lifting, and Simon pulled at the wet tunic
that clung to his skin. He was lying in a pool of sweat, and he
longed to be out of his moist bed. It was then that he realized that
his body didn't hurt as it had before. When he tested his strength by
lifting his arm, he was still weak as a newborn lamb, but something
was changing for the better.

Ha! He wasn't the weak milksop they all thought him to be after
all . . . his family, all filling his house and eating his food and waiting for his demise. Not this time! People said things when a man was
sick and helpless that they would quail even to think when he was
healthy. They revealed attitudes that were best hidden when a man
was well. There were lapses in judgment. And the shameful neglect
his wife showed him . . .

"Wife! Woman!"

His voice was stronger now, too, and he could feel his senses returning. How long had he been in bed like this? How long had he been wasting away? A couple days? A couple weeks? Months, perhaps? He couldn't tell. One day had bled into another.

Now he could hear her footsteps approaching, and he rolled his head so that he could see her when she entered the room. She arrived with her hands white with flour and her sleeves tied back to expose the jiggling softness of her upper arms. Her robe hung expertly over the ample mounds of her body, and her graying hair was tied back with a thong so that her head looked smaller than it should. Her eyes were wide and terror-stricken, and she paused in the doorway with one foot in the air like an overfed chicken. The sudden mental image made him want to laugh. What came out was a wheezy snort.

"Yes, husband?" she asked quietly. "You called for me?"

"I'm as wet as a drowned mouse," he snapped. "Can't you see?"

Kneeling next to him, she pulled his covers back. The air of the room felt chilly against his moist skin, and he shivered.

"Your fever seems to have broken," she said in awe. "Simon, you are getting better!"

The surprise in her voice was insulting, and had he not been so focused on his own discomfort, he might have made her regret it. As it was, he clawed at his tunic, trying to pull it away from his skin. He could smell his own musty scent, and wondered if he repulsed her.

But she didn't seem to be put off, and she pulled him forward with her strong arms and tugged the tunic off his body. Then taking another cloth, she began to rub his skin, drying him thoroughly. But the moment he was dry, his flesh began to sweat again.

Trying to stay upright so that she could dry his back was exhausting, and he let himself fall back, feeling his wife's fingers caught between his body and the floor. Ordinarily he would have rolled slightly to release her, but he didn't this time. Her strong, soft arm was under him, and her warm, sweet-smelling body was so near him. He leaned his head toward her bosom and let it rest there. It was the most comfort he had felt in a long, long time. He felt almost as if his own mother were holding him.

Yardena was motionless, her breath suspended. Slowly he felt her begin to breathe again, but she seemed to be doing so warily. He'd been a difficult patient, he knew. Had said things she didn't deserve when he thought he was dying and wouldn't have to face those words again. But now he wasn't dying.

A man did not say he was sorry, though. Never apologize to a woman, let alone one's wife! He did not say he was wrong. A man was always 10 times more right on his worst day than a woman was on her best day. An apology was not in order. Instead, he said, "Don't let that lump of a girl, Martha, touch the bread. She ruins it every time. Your bread is better."

"Oh." She said it like a sigh, and then she slowly lowered her cheek to rest on the top of his head.

But still he had more on his conscience than the bellowing he had done at his wife. There were the words his niece had spoken when he tried to give her advice about her unmarried state. The things she had said . . . as if a man could be held accountable for women's foibles! Eve had begun it all long ago, and man could not be blamed if woman degraded herself.

Martha blamed him, though—blamed him for Mary and for herself, too. But he had seen what Mary really was when she was only a child. And time had proved him right! It was Mary who had tarnished him! She had tainted his righteousness with her wicked, womanly filth.

But something inside of him was still not easy.

"Get better now, husband," Yardena said softly. "Rest and let your body gain strength. I will get some water to bathe you if you feel ready."

"Go," he ordered. His voice didn't hold the authority he had hoped for. It sounded more like a plea, and he grimaced at the sound.

When she tugged at her hand, still trapped under his body, he shifted reluctantly. He could never allow her to know what comfort those strong, jiggling arms brought him this day. No, she would let it go to her head and think that he required her for his happiness. And that would be wrong.

Now he would do something big—would show them all that he was still alive and that he still mattered. Simon would throw a big party—would invite the most influential . . . the healer! That's whom he would invite. That healer whom Lazarus was so proud to be associated with. The healer that had raised his young nephew from the dead. Now he would demonstrate to the entire village that not only Lazarus could associate with the preacher, but he could too. He'd always been slightly jealous of Lazarus. Jesus seemed to have a true regard for the nitwit of a boy. (And, though he did not want to think about it, perhaps he needed to do something to smooth over the messy confrontation he had participated in at the Temple. But he instantly pushed that out of his mind.)

Yes, Simon would show him what a true dinner consisted of. It would be cooked by Yardena, not that dried-up spinster Martha. And everyone had to admit that Yardena was an excellent cook. Jesus would note the difference.

Hadn't Jesus healed him two years before? He doubted that He would even remember. People were cured just by brushing against the man. Simon would not remind him of that healing, though. No, it was not best to bring it back to public memory. Leprosy was foul and loathsome. Sometimes Simon still had nightmares of being back in the leper colony and unable to escape. He dreamed of the stench—that rotting, stinking odor of decay on one's own body. No, leprosy was something best left in the past. The village must not be reminded of it, especially after he had been so ill. They must see the power oozing from him, the respectability wafting around him like a cloud. The community must look up to glimpse his face, and then stare back down to the dirt in shame.

Yes, he was becoming himself again as he regained his strength—he could feel it! And there was one more thing he must do: he must summon the rest of the family and demonstrate that he still had the power of a patriarch in this clan. He'd show them . . .

Earlier today his daughters had come to visit him. Shiloh, so round and happy, had always been exuberant. It had melted his heart to see her so happy. Tisha had always been thinner, as her mother had been for so many years. She was also more serious, with a greater tendency toward a sharp tongue. He hoped she didn't use it on her husband. Of course, the young women would never be so casual around their father, but what they didn't realize was that he had eavesdropped as they had talked in the kitchen. When the women thought he was sleeping, he lay alone listening to their voices. At first it had been difficult to make out what they were saying, but it seemed that the fever enhanced his hearing, and he could make out snatches of conversation. A woman's world was a peculiar thing. Such a petty environment. Nothing of importance in it. He wondered how women managed to enjoy it in any way at all. But that was the role of a woman, and she was born into it. She didn't think like a man. It was her God-given place, wasn't it?

Now his sons had made him proud. His eldest, Jacob, was strong and decided. He would not let anything push him around. Simon trusted him implicitly. Jacob had learned well from him. Respecting his father, he valued Simon's opinions and suggestions. Yes, Jacob was a good son.

Rashan was another type of man. The younger son who would not inherit, he kept his own counsel. Of course, Rashan never went against his father's word, but he also didn't solicit suggestions. His reticence had been frustrating at times, but Simon had no real reason to be unhappy with the boy. He was betrothed to be married, and someday soon he would go and claim his bride. But she was still young, and it would be two or three years before she was old enough to be a proper wife. Simon was satisfied with the prospective marriage, however. She came from a good family—she would be a decent wife.

Why was it that his daughters were the ones to bring him comfort at a time like this? Women! Such a frustrating gender in general, and so difficult to live with. One had to have a hand of iron with a woman. If one did not perpetually keep her in her place, she was always trying to squirm back out of it. But when a man was sick, it somehow warmed him to see his daughters' tenderness toward him.

His wife was another story. A good wife, she worked hard and knew her place. She never defied him openly (albeit in sneaky and subtle ways she did). But he imagined most women did that. Yes, she was good, but Yardena had never been his choice. He'd asked his father for a girl named Anna—so pretty and petite. With her big, innocent eyes, no girl looked more ravishing holding her water jug than Anna did. His father, however, had other plans. He chose Yardena for Simon because her father's fields adjoined his own, and because while she was big-boned and hearty, she was very well connected socially. Not known for her delicate looks, Yardena was sufficiently well off to make her desirable for the family. Simon had not argued. That was out of the question. A father's word was law! But he had not been happy with his father's choice until Anna died while giving birth to her first child—a girl. Only then did Simon see his father's wisdom in selecting a hearty wife. A strong wife did not die easily—and had sons!

Even so, Yardena was not Anna, and he could not forget this. It wasn't that she was a bad wife. Not at all! But his irritation with her grew through the years. She did not have Anna's silken curls, which he had spied once when her veil had slipped. Yardena's hair was coarse and lusterless. Nor did she have Anna's petite figure—she was big-boned and physically strong. And Yardena did not have Anna's delightful laugh, one that tinkled like the bells at the bottom of a priest's robe. As the years passed, his frustration with her only intensified. The more he shouted, the harder she tried to please him. Until one day she stopped and simply did her duty and no more.

Where was that water to bathe him? In time she would come, he knew, bringing it and another blanket. Perhaps she would have some broth or boiled meat. But she would take her time. He wondered if it was her way of revenge. Was she taking out on him years of spite that had built up? But what did she have to be spiteful about? He was a well-respected, handsome man! She'd been the lucky one in the marriage arrangement.

The distant murmur of the women in the kitchen reached him. Martha would be there. She was always in the kitchen. Irritating was what she was. Her actions were always so correct—not a bit of softness about her. And Mary . . . was Mary there? She would be silent if she were. None of the others would talk to her. A wave of disgust swept over him at the thought of her.

She was filthy, that girl! He knew it. Mary had been filthy since she was just a small child, something he'd sensed in her very early. It was because of her that he had sinned! If it hadn't been for her, he would have been a perfectly righteous man, following all of God's decrees.

It had been the idea of more influential men to trap her in adultery. He had volunteered to set the trap, claiming that she would trust him more. And it was true. She had thought she owned him—thought the secret she held kept her safe from him. But she was wrong!

"It will be a test that Jesus will not be able to escape!" one of the leading Pharisees had insisted. "He will have to admit that she must be punished. There will be no way around it! And when she is punished and killed before his face, we will demand why he associates with such sinners, and then bring witnesses that he befriends prostitutes and vagabonds."

She'd be killed. At first he had felt a sudden rush of revulsion at the idea, but the more he thought about it, the more he realized it was his only way out! When she was stoned to death, his weakness would die with her.

He feared, however, that he had volunteered to trap her a little too quickly. What if the men wondered why he would want to do such a thing? What if they pieced everything together? But with her dead, and their trap for Jesus successful, all would be well again. All would be well . . .

Mary would be stoned. While it would be ugly and unpleasant, afterward the village would see that justice had been done. People would then publicly forget about her. It would be as if she had never been born. The men who had paid for her services, and those who had induced her through other means, would be able to put their sins behind them. No one would look into the past anymore. It would only be the present—a present without *her*.

And Simon would be free. He would live an even more holy life, attending synagogue more often than he did now, would wake up even earlier to pray, and would associate with only the holiest of men. Then he would stop feeling as if he had somehow failed, when it wasn't his failure at all, but the wickedness of one woman!

She was yours to protect, but you used her instead. That was what Jesus had traced on the courtyard pavement before Simon turned away. Jesus had written some other things first. Stolen land will yield no harvest. The children of servants kill their masters. Other men had read and turned away. Obviously Jesus had seen something inside of them. Simon wondered what their hidden sins had been. But he dared not delve into other men's secret sins if he wanted to protect his own!

Surely Jesus was a prophet. To know such things!

"Jesus is a friend of gossips!" the high priest had assured him. "There are no secrets in a village, no matter how a man tries to hide things."

Perhaps he'd been right. Secrets did not stay hidden. They had a way of worming their way out of their rightful places. Like women, he noted with a wry smile.

The healer refused to follow the social rules—that was His problem! He needed someone like Simon to show Him how these things worked, someone who understood social codes and etiquette. How could a carpenter grasp such things? Simon would support Him. He would reach down and bring Jesus up to a level that He only imagined! Then the healer would be popular among the influential as well, and perhaps then He would stop insulting the more educated.

"I've been a good man!" Simon murmured to himself. "I've been a good man!"

And he was a good man. He was a Pharisee. Everyone in the village would tell you how holy he was. All his friends would sing his praises from the rooftops! Even his enemies could not deny how much money he had given to the Temple program. And now he would support this preacher with the strange healing powers.

Simon was a good man. A bad man would not be so selfless, would he?

CHAPTER 15

"All at once he followed her like an ox going to the slaughter, like a deer stepping into a noose."

PROVERBS 7:22

Jebuseh shook his head and frowned.

"Too low!" he declared. "I would be losing money if I sold you the cloth for so little. It is wrong to rob your own neighbor, friend!"

"You ask too much!" the man argued. "Your fabric may be the best quality in these parts, but your price is too high!"

His hands behind his back, Jebuseh silently waited. Gray heavily streaked his beard, and he now began to rock back and forth on his heels as he watched his customer fingering the fabric. He knew the quality of his work, and he knew the price he could ask. Jebuseh was no fool.

"I cannot lower it, friend," he said finally. He made a show of frowning. "But you are my neighbor. For you, I will make a deal. But only for you! For anyone else, I would refuse."

Money exchanged hands, and the merchant laid the fabric, carefully wrapped in an old piece of cloth, across the back of his customer's donkey.

"God be with you, friend!" Jebuseh said. "Give my best to your lovely wife."

His business doing well, Jebuseh had no complaints. God had abundantly blessed his finances. The village considered him a wealthy man (and could afford as much food as he wanted, as his ample belly testified to the whole community), and he had not gotten to this place by cheating anyone. Proud of the fact that he had been honest, he had always measured squarely, and he never overcharged. Even today he had given this man a cheaper price than he knew he could demand. But he did not need the extra money, and he did not want to deny his neighbor good fabric. The man's wife would be overjoyed to see its quality. A married man, he knew the pleasure a woman could take in small luxuries.

Jebuseh's business had belonged to his father before him, and the son had worked alongside the father until the old man died. At that time Jebuseh took the business over and continued building its already-substantial client base. Of course, there were always friends and family who faithfully bought his finely woven fabrics, but friends and family married and had children. Families sometimes migrated elsewhere, and word of Jebuseh's superior quality had spread as far as Jerusalem. Even further, he had heard.

Yes indeed, God had blessed! There was no other way to explain it. The Lord rewarded his honesty and devotion. But He had not given him an heir. Who would take on the family business? Would it pass to the children of his brothers? That was not right. He should have children of his own—an heir of his own.

Lilar . . . his wife. She was a good woman, but she could not bear children. God had closed her womb. Poor Lilar, who had prayed and prayed for children of her own. A wife who had worked tirelessly by his side, supporting him with her love and faithful hard work, she was a good woman. He could never complain about her. Except for the lack of children.

It was hard for him to make the suggestion. She had looked at him, her eyes swimming with emotions that her weathered cheeks refused to betray.

"I must have an heir, my wife," he tried to explain. "Who will take my name? Who will continue this business we have worked so hard to build?"

Lilar had been silent.

"A second wife would be below you," he went on. "A second wife would do as you told her. You would still be mistress. The children born would be like your own. You could raise them!"

Was this true in reality? He was not so sure. But the decision was not hers to make. It was his. If he desired a second wife, he would take one. Yet he did not want to hurt her—not Lilar, the woman who had nursed him through fevers and awakened before him every day of their 25-year marriage to light the fire and start his breakfast. While he was the man of the home, he also had 25 years of experience in marriage. It had taught him that if your wife was not happy, no matter how strong and in control you were, you were not happy, either. That was wisdom acquired over 25 years, and he did not want to bring disharmony into his home. No, that would not do.

Eventually Lilar had agreed. She could not give him children, and she knew it. Reluctantly she had given her blessing, asking only that he permit her to help choose the woman. And after a long silent time of thinking, Lilar had chosen Martha.

Why Martha? He did not know. Perhaps because she was plain, and his wife was not afraid that he would lust after the younger woman too much. Women were such a jealous lot. Martha was known for her hard work and the fact that she did not shirk duty. Whatever the reason, his wife had approved of Lazarus' sister.

How could his wife have known that his discomfort about Martha was bound up with her sister? It was not only that the family had a prostitute in its midst—it was that he had known that prostitute. She had been his particular weakness. Although he had always been a God-fearing man, like his ancestor David he had fallen in weakness to a seductive woman. It was the woman's fault for being the way she was—for luring him away from the faithful embrace of his wife! He had not visited her many times. His conscience soon made him break the relationship. But the memory of what he had done remained . . . the memory that his wife did not know of.

Yes, he still remembered Mary—and with guilt and regret. And now he was arranging to marry her sister.

God, why don't You answer Your servant?

It was his usual prayer, since the God of Israel would not answer his questions or provide him guidance. He would not tell him if Martha were the right choice for a second wife or not. God remained silent. Why would He not point out the woman to bear his children? Although He had led in every other aspect of his life, God seemed to have removed Himself from this decision of which woman should become his second wife. Jebuseh did not understand.

He had put off Lazarus as much as possible, although he hated to do it. Lazarus was a good, honest man. Although Jebuseh had nearly solidified the arrangement, something still held him back. Perhaps a suggestion made by Jacob, Lazarus' cousin, caused him to hesitate.

It was something that would go against dear Lilar's wishes. But he was the man of this house! He was the one in charge, was he not? And he knew best!

Or did he?

What was the right path? Which woman would be the proper wife to bear him children? Who was the one that would bring harmony and children's laughter into his home?

God of our fathers, why do You remain silent?

Lilar would have poured her heart out to her mother if she were still alive. As it was, Lilar was old enough to be a grandmother had she had a child of her own. And a wise woman kept her own counsel. She didn't reveal her emotions for the village to gawk at.

It was midmorning as she stood perfectly still before the two-storied dwelling, her lips pursed in uncertainty. The breeze had picked up, bringing the afternoon heat with it, and Lilar could feel a trickle of sweat sliding down her side. Her body was not what it used to be, her belly having grown and her skin sagging. A pouch of skin under her chin reminded her of her old grandmother. Her legs were no longer shapely. But there was still beauty in age, was there not? Beauty still lingered under these wrinkles—beauty in years spent together.

Jebuseh did not deny this. Yet he still required a second wife.

She raised her fist to knock before she had time to change her mind. It was taking a chance that anyone would be home at all. The family would be with Simon, who, rumor had it, was dying. If anyone would be here, it would be Martha. But if someone else answered her knock?

Holding her breath, Lilar pulled her veil up around her face, leaving only one eye free. The dust was blowing hard, and she could feel the dryness of it begin to settle into her scalp. She glanced up at the house. It was well built, with upper sleeping quarters. Several goats were tied up beside it, and a cursory glance shrewdly told her that they were well cared for and amply fed. No scabs or lesions on those animals.

The sound of movement came from inside, and when the door began to creak open, Lilar felt a childish urge to run away. But she stood her ground.

Martha looked surprised to see her, Lilar noted with grim satisfaction. The young woman's eyes widened, and although she had been about to lower her veil to her shoulders as one woman does when conversing with another in her own doorway, she abruptly paused. Martha's features were not delicate, and lines had already begun to form on her brows and between her lips and her nose. Her eyes were small, and she narrowed them further, obviously trying to decide what to do.

"Is anyone else home?" Lilar asked hurriedly.

Instead of answering audibly, Martha shook her head, and Lilar nodded confidently.

"Good. Then we can talk."

Bullying would do no good on this one. Martha obviously had

a spine and a brain. She was watching Lilar alertly, and she did not automatically step back to let Lilar into her home.

"This is not customary," Martha said carefully.

"No, it is not. That is why I would be grateful if you would let me inside and out of public view."

Conceding, Martha stepped backward, allowing Lilar to slip inside with one backward glance. The house was well kept. Clean and neat, it smelled of cooking, and nothing seemed rancid. Lilar gave it grudging approval.

"Are we alone?" she asked quietly.

"Entirely. Come, I will get you some water."

Without a backward glance Martha headed toward the kitchen area. Was it her age, or was there something threatening even in this plain, stolid young woman before her? She'd thought that Martha, of all women, would not be a rival for her husband's love, but watching the woman move tempted her to change her mind. Martha still had good hips and moved with more grace than Lilar had remembered. She seemed confident in her own body and was more of a threat than Lilar had expected.

Dipping a pitcher into a large storage jar, Martha poured the contents into an earthen cup. She passed it wordlessly to Lilar, then crossed her arms. Lilar noted that the younger woman had not taken off her veil. It gave her a sense of security, the older woman recognized. Lilar also kept her veil raised.

"My husband has selected you as a possible second wife," she began. "We shouldn't wander around the well, but get straight to the point."

"It is good of your husband to see value in me," Martha said diplomatically.

"Do you work hard?"

"What else does an old maid like me do with herself?"

"And your health? It is good?"

"Yes."

"I will be first wife. My word will be law. You realize that?"

"Yes." Martha's voice seemed to have no malice in it.

"We can get along if we want to. We can be friends."

Martha looked down uncertainly. "It will be an awkward situation for some time," she said slowly. "I don't pretend it won't be. But you are first wife, and I would be only second."

"Little happiness has ever graced a home with more than one mistress."

"Why have you come?" Martha asked, ignoring the comment.

"To see what you are up close. I wanted to find out what kind of woman will possibly be living with me." *And my husband*, she thought to herself.

"You hate this."

"Would you not in my situation?" Lilar almost laughed. "Yes, young miss, I hate this!"

"Are you wanting to discourage me?"

"If it isn't you, it will be another. An heir is important. I want an understanding between us women. Left to men, they think a marriage will sort itself out. That is very misguided."

"And what agreement would you like?" Martha asked.

"That I will be mistress. That you will obey me as you would your mother. That once you are pregnant, you will put your energy and emotion into your child and leave my husband to me."

My husband. Had she given herself away? She loved him and did not want to share him. And looking at this young, albeit plain, woman, she felt the venom in her rising.

"I am too old to be considered marriageable," Martha said, clutching her hands together so tightly that her knuckles were white. Lilar watched those work-roughened hands as Martha spoke. "I have no family of my own. I have a brother who is married, and I am very much in the way here. I know it, but something inside of me won't let me give up my place here. A marriage, even to be the second wife, is better than to be unmarried forever. I am willing to do what I need to in order to keep peace in my new home. A child is more than I could hope for in this house, is it not? If you will leave me to love and raise my children, I will not interfere with . . ." Here she paused. ". . . our husband."

Our husband. Lilar hated the sound of it. She wondered how she would possibly survive this. It was definitely not ideal. In fact, it was not even remotely acceptable. But a man did what he did. She could not stop him. He wanted an heir, and she could not blame him for trying to get one. After all, she had failed to give him any children. Could she live with this Martha? Could they coexist together and not fight like feral cats? If the woman knew her place, they just might.

This was a mistake. Lilar could feel the truth of it as solidly as she felt the cool earth under her feet. Martha was not one to be cowed. She would not bend for an old woman. No, she would take what she wanted, as would any young woman with a chance at a life and a family. And the elderly would be left behind—a decaying memory.

And softly, like a moth fluttering toward an oil lamp, Lilar realized that she wanted to die. It was a gentle realization. Suddenly she wanted to die and let her husband move on if he must. But she could not live in the same house where her husband had children with another woman. Having all of her husband's attention all these long years had spoiled her. She had grown accustomed to his love and gentleness—had grown possessive of his tender ways.

Lilar gave Martha a faraway smile.

I am defeated, she thought. If she let go of his love, she would lay down and die. She knew it. If she fought to keep his affection, she would turn into something jealous and venomous. What was her choice? Only God gave death to His servants. No, she must plod on. Must fight for the man she loved and see what kind of woman she turned into.

Martha stood at her doorway, watching the retreating form of Lilar—the woman who would be fellow wife to her . . . who would share her new husband and would try to thwart her at every turn. She knew this well enough. Lilar had not come to find common ground or discover a way to have a harmonious home. No, she had hoped to find Martha's weakness.

Standing next to the solid wooden door, Martha rested her arm on the crossbar that at night secured it from the inside. She could feel the dust drifting past her in the faint wind, scattering behind her into her clean house. Her house . . . would it be her house much longer? It would be up to Rachel to take care of it soon. But it would never be as clean as she kept it.

Part of her felt her own strength. Perhaps she had never been beautiful, but she had power that she hadn't before realized—a power that this old woman feared. Martha—plain, hardworking Martha—was a woman to be reckoned with. Not accustomed to this kind of feeling, she stood motionless, memorizing it carefully. It was like the strange weight of a sword in the hand of a common villager. While the sword was heavy and cumbersome, some instinct assured its bearer that it might prove important at a later time.

Would she leave the man to his first wife? She was not sure. Would she be happy with having the children, and allotting the personal care of their husband to the other woman? Or would she rise up and seize it all?

It seemed so real now. She'd been afraid to hope before . . . had been disappointed too many times in the past. But if the other wife was coming to see what kind of woman she was . . . if the negotiations had come so far . . . perhaps the delay was just a matter of money. Perhaps the men were debating a dowry or establishing the rights that the second wife could expect.

Lilar wouldn't have come otherwise, would she? She wouldn't have risked being seen if Martha were only a possible second wife. No, she would only come if the decision were all but made!

Martha, daughter of Moseh, would no longer be known by that name. She would be Martha, wife of Jebuseh. Less-loved wife? Wife of convenience for the sake of an heir? Did it matter? Wife! She would be a wife. Finally, she would be respected by all as a full woman!

It was finally happening. Martha smiled to herself. No longer would she be the woman helping other women prepare for something. And she would no longer be the one provided for out of family duty. She would truly belong, would be taken seriously. Other women would have to admit grudging respect. And it was finally happening to her.

As Martha looked out over the village she could see the last of the poor women and servant girls making their morning trip to the well. Her gaze followed the worn path with the stones worn smooth from

generations of feet and the scraggly fig trees that offered brief and fluttering shade. She could smell the dry dust in the air and the distant
scent of cooking fires and the sharp tang of goat dung from the
nearby milk goats that bleated quietly to each other. Flies bumped
lazily against her hands, and she batted them away.

Remember this moment and cherish it, she thought to herself.
Someday she would tell her daughters about the time she could feel
the world changing in her favor.

Martha, wife of Jebuseh. It had a nice ring to it. If she had doubts
before about the potential happiness of the union, they had vanished
now. Happiness was the respect of the village. Happiness was the
recognition of the other women. Happiness lay in the children she
would give birth to.

Loving a husband too much only led to heartbreak. It was better to be pleasantly disinterested in the man and adore the children.
Martha would not do anything differently than any of the women
before her. Plodding the path they had worn for her, she would join
their ranks and wish for nothing more.

Martha would be a wife.

CHAPTER 16

*"Daughters of Jerusalem, I charge you by the gazelles and by the
does of the field: Do not arouse or awaken love until it so desires."*

SONG OF SONGS 3:5

He is dying, I'd say," the small, dusty girl said, her lips pursed in
an expression too adult for her small body. A water jug balanced on her shoulder, and she eased it down to the ground with a
hollow thud. She began to wind some rags around her hands, giving her full attention to the task.

"Think so?" the other asked, her eyes widening with interest.
"You shouldn't speak of it, though."

"No, maybe not. But it's true. If it were one of my family, I shouldn't say anything, but since it's *them* . . ."

She said the word with meaning. Them. It was always a battle between "people like us" and "our betters." Simon was her better, but in her opinion, he was really not so much better than her own family was. She tested her bound palms and made a satisfied sound in the back of her throat. The two serving girls stood by the well, their water jugs waiting. But getting water was not simply a necessary task. It was also a time to chat and gossip, to relax and let down their guards ever so little.

"He called for a family meeting," the little girl said, giving a significant nod—the motion an old woman might use when gossiping with other widows. "Everyone—your house, too."

The other girl, taller and a little older, inhaled quickly. There was drama to come—she could smell it in the air. They were only servant girls, but they weren't stupid. One was a servant in Simon's house, and the other in Lazarus' house. Sometimes it felt as if the two of them knew more than the two households combined!

"To tell his last words, then?" the taller girl asked. She crossed her well-muscled arms over her thin chest.

"Might be. I'll listen as much as I can."

"If he dies, what happens to you?"

"They'll keep me on, I'm sure. Jacob will be much wealthier with his father's inheritance. They can afford two or three of us!"

Both girls lapsed into silence. The smaller one had thrown the pot, attached to a long rope, down into the mouth of the well, and it clattered against the stones lining it. When the rope went slack, she began to haul it expertly upward, pulling evenly, hand over hand, until the pot emerged into the sparkling sunlight and she poured its cold contents into her large water jar.

Something important was about to happen. They knew it. It would be worth gossiping about for days, maybe even weeks! But it would not change things for them. No, they knew their place, their lot in life. They would remain in the families they had been serving since they were small girls, cooking, cleaning, and fetching water. And they would continue to gossip about the wealthy families they worked for.

Pot after pot emerged, brimming with water from the depths of the well.

"Funerals are hard work," the smaller girl complained. "So many people bathing and eating and drinking."

Her companion gave a sympathetic grunt as she heaved the earthenware jug to her shoulder.

"So many feet to wash," she sighed. "So many requests for food—the food is never enough! And the washing up after the cooking . . ."

"Not yet, though," her friend reminded her.

"God willing! Maybe the guests will all leave soon, and let the old man recover!"

They turned their heavy footsteps toward the well-worn path that led from the well, their jugs balanced carefully on their young shoulders. As they moved with practiced agility over the bumpy trail, they sighed over the hardworking life of a servant.

The well had allowed momentary release from the daily drudgery. Soon they would be back at the homes they served, and they would have to swallow all such complaints.

The family had gathered in an atmosphere of expectation. More people than ever were sitting nearly on top of each other in the living area of Simon's home. Shoulder to shoulder, they greeted each other with subdued enthusiasm. The women spilled out of the kitchen area, and Martha, her back against the smooth, plastered wall, surveyed the people before her.

Jacob was there, and she could hear Erda's voice from somewhere. Their children were playing outdoors with the other children. Jacob was still a handsome man, but Martha had stopped wondering what life would have been like as his wife. Some things, like girlish hopes, were best left in the past.

Shiloh's and Tisha's husbands were also present, talking in low voices with Lazarus, their arms crossed over their chests, and their eyes rising to glance around in slight anxiety. Still other cousins talked and nodded. Some of the women stood in a small knot to the side, unable to get into the crowded kitchen area. Children peered inside through the door, and when their chatter got to be too loud, adults shooed them back out to play farther away.

Martha stood next to her sister. She felt self-conscious being so close to Mary. A part of her wanted as much distance as possible from her younger sibling—from the rumors, from the disapproval, from the sideways glances. She leaned imperceptively away, and tried to still the anxiety that welled up inside of her. But she was not alone in her feeling as she felt tension throughout the house—she was only one thread in a family tapestry being pulled and strained. Death was not easy—preparing for it was possibly more difficult than dealing with the finality of it. But family made things easier to bear. The group could sustain a greater burden than an individual. Together they would cope with their multitude of emotions concerning old Uncle Simon. Most silently recognized that there would not be unanimous grief.

"I wonder what Uncle Simon wanted," Mary murmured.

Martha gave her sister a quick glance. Mary looked tired and worn. Rejection, Martha realized, was an exhausting state to endure. Her own eyes had faint rings beneath them, and the lines in her face were more pronounced.

"I don't know." Martha took a deep breath. "But Jacob seems to have gone in to him."

They both looked in the direction of the room Uncle Simon was using as a bedroom. It was safer for him to be on the lower level of the house than the upper level, where the stairs might prove too much.

"I hate this," Mary said softly. "The waiting . . ."

"I know." Martha gave her sister a sympathetic glance.

Waiting. They were waiting for an uncle's pronouncement—waiting for an uncle's death. And after his death they would wait for the appropriate mourning period to end. The waiting did not end, but just bled into another time of waiting.

Just then they heard rustling, some murmuring, and a few sharp words from Uncle Simon through the wall. Jacob emerged from the room, carefully supporting his father, one arm around his back, and a hand tucked under his armpit. The old man had shrunk during the past few weeks, and being a big man himself, Jacob's only challenge seemed to be to transport his father gently enough. He moved slowly and carefully, his face showing deep concern. The old man muttered irritably as he settled into a sitting position with pillows all around. He didn't look as sick anymore, and Martha couldn't help wondering, with dread curdling her stomach, if the old man weren't recovering by some miracle. Simon seemed focused on something inward instead of the people gathered in front of him. His son leaned down and whispered into his father's ear.

"I know, I know!" Simon said, batting him away with a weak arm. Jacob backed up, but looked ready to lunge forward at the least sign of alarm.

"I am not well," Simon began in his cracked voice. His voice was still soft and barely above a whisper, and his family leaned forward, hushing each other so they could hear.

"I am not well," he repeated quietly, his eyes again seeming to look inward. "I have done my best for all of you . . ."

He did not finish the sentence. Martha leaned forward, frowning.

"My son, Jacob . . . if anything should happen to me, he will take my place as the head of this family. You will grant him the respect you have always given me. But that has not happened yet, and I am feeling much stronger now. You will be happy to know that I am recovering."

Surprised exclamations and praises sent up to God rippled across the crowded room. Martha knew that many of them lacked sincerity, but if the old man recovered, this was not a time for honest reaction. Simon looked tired, and did not try to talk over the voices. He waited until they had quieted before he spoke again.

"I have other pleasant news for you," he went on, his old face crinkling into a smile of satisfaction. "A small bout of sickness doesn't stop me from arranging for this family as my duty requires."

Some laughter and nods greeted his words.

"I have a special occasion to announce to all of you. There is a man in our community . . . a good man. A sound man. He has shown interest in joining with us in the bonds of family."

The women let out excited whispers at this, then hurriedly hushed each other, pressing into the room to hear better.

"The man's name is Jebuseh, a prosperous businessman recognized for his quality fabrics. You all know him, and I have approved his request. He is welcome in our family. He will be good to his new kin. He will bring us honor!"

Martha, her heart pounding, schooled her features into a calm expression. A woman did not betray her emotions, no matter how much she wanted to. An honorable woman did not let those around her know that her breathing was shallow and her hands shook. She looked down, feeling her cheeks grow warm in a blush of pleasure.

Old Uncle Simon, with all his bad qualities, was perhaps not so bad after all. He was arranging a marriage for her, giving his blessing, showing the family the honor of her new position. His approval amounted to that of the family at large. Something close to fondness rose up in her heart, and she felt her eyes misting with tears.

"I am happy to announce the finalized betrothal of our new brother Jebuseh," Uncle Simon went on, "and our very own Mahzala!"

As the happy cheer went up, a young woman in the kitchen received excited congratulations and hugs from the women. Martha stood in complete stillness. Mahzala. Her young cousin. *Nineteen, the girl was, and definitely high time she was married.* That was what they all thought, wasn't it? But what about her? Martha had waited patiently—had done her duty. Cooking and caring for her brother, she had done every last thing expected of her!

Anger flooded through her veins, and her lips became a thin line. Mahzala—the younger woman who could have married any number of other men . . . could have married a man her age with no difficulty! She did not have her age counting against her like a fatal flaw . . . had a pretty face and bright eyes. Mahzala!

It was over. As quickly as that, all her hopes for this marriage were dashed. Life would return to its same dusty patterns of a few weeks ago. Martha would not be a wife. No, she would continue to be Martha, sister of Lazarus, daughter of Moseh. She would be the dependable old maid of the family, doing her duty and celebrating everyone else's good fortune. Doomed to smile and accept her lot and endure the shame.

Her head lowered so that no one could see the emotions betrayed in her eyes, she slipped through the crowd of family . . . pushed against their shoulders and headed for the door leading outside.

Escape! It was all she could think of. And the women clucked their tongues and murmured, "Jealous of her own cousin's good fortune!"

"Understandable at her age," another pointed out.

"It doesn't mean that another must share her fate!"

"She should be happy for her cousin! It is a bad spirit to show displeasure at a time of happiness for the family!"

"So kind of dear Simon to arrange such a lucrative marriage for a girl so young! Only a man of his wisdom would have been able to arrange such a match."

Yes, dear, kind Uncle Simon . . .

Lazarus sighed and rubbed his eyes. He had worked hard for this match for his sister—had put his energy into it as if it were his own marriage! If anyone deserved that union, it was Martha. Too many times she had been passed over. It was her turn. And her brother—the man who was supposed to be her protector and provider—had failed her.

"Congratulations," Lazarus said absently, giving what he hoped was a sincere smile to the girl's brother. "She'll make a wonderful wife!"

And really, could Lazarus blame Jebuseh for wanting a younger, prettier girl? Yes, part of him could. Jebuseh was an old man already. A match between an old man and a young girl was not good. Especially to be second wife to an old man! But for Martha, it would have been as good as she could expect. She would have worked harder than Mahzala. Not as spoiled, she would have caused less friction in the home. Was this not what Jebuseh had professed only a week ago?

It was good that Lazarus hadn't spoken of the match, had hidden it. It saved him the embarrassment of facing his whole family as a failure.

"Boy!"

It was Uncle Simon, his weak voice rising as much as it could into a reedy whine. As Lazarus turned toward the old man, his heart slowly filled with fury. It was not Jebuseh who had thwarted him—it was his uncle!

"Soon you should manage a marriage for those two sisters of yours," Simon said, his eyes filled with amusement.

Lazarus did not reply.

"Getting a little long in the tooth, eh?" the old man chuckled to himself weakly.

It took all of his self-control to swallow his bitter answer. But Uncle Simon was still the head of his family, an elder to be respected. One girl in the family had been provided for, and what did it matter to old Simon which one it was? The uncle was not a man to be spoken sharply to. A nephew did not disrespect his uncle.

"I have done my best, Uncle," Lazarus said quietly.

"Your best, eh?"

"Perhaps, Uncle, you could aid me in the search for suitable husbands for my sisters," he said, his voice low and controlled. "You are a well-respected man, and your word goes much further than my own."

Simon threw him a narrowed, calculating glance, but then seemed to disregard any implied malice in the words. He shrugged his shoulders.

"Perhaps Jacob may do so after me. I am old and tired." Simon coughed heavily, and as he did so, Lazarus took the opportunity to turn away.

Respect meant that Lazarus could not confront his uncle. Respect meant that Lazarus must not question his uncle. Respect called for Lazarus to be indulgent of an old man, because one day Lazarus too would be elderly. One day he too would have children to humor him in his moods.

The patriarch always knew best. He was leading a family, and that meant he could not favor one over another. The patriarch must not be questioned. After all, he had lived a long time. Although Simon might seem to be insulting, perhaps Lazarus deserved some derision. He had not done well by his sisters.

Lazarus rubbed his eyes again. The most difficult part was that he could not call upon his family for support. Here he was, surrounded by family, and he could not turn to them—could not tell them what had happened. Yet it was the purpose of family to be a network of support when one needed them—to give one a place of belonging . . . an identity . . .

O God, he prayed. *I have failed! Forgive me for my inability to provide proper husbands for my sisters. O God, do not punish them for my weakness. In Your strength, provide for them!*

The feelings of anger and disgust he felt toward the pathetic old man who ruled their family could not be put into words. They could not be included in a prayer! No, he must quash them. It was wrong of him even to think them.

CHAPTER 17

"For there is a proper time and procedure for every matter, though a man's misery weighs heavily upon him."

ECCLESIASTES 8:6

As Martha escaped into the open air, she took a deep breath and willed her tears to stop. Simon had done this purposefully—he'd warned her, hadn't he, that he would ruin her life if she spoke . . . that she would regret it . . .

And she did. She wished now that she had kept her mouth shut, just doing her duty and ignoring her uncle's past sins. If only she had looked out for her own happiness instead of for the pain her sister had endured as a girl. The past was the past, was it not? Why had she delved into it?

The perfect amount of rainfall that had blessed the land during the rainy season now promised a bountiful crop of olives. The gray-green groves had always been a source of peace for Martha. As a girl, she had known that Jacob was in those groves, working for his father. The sun had glistened off his dark curls, and his tan deepened as he bent under his work. And she had hoped for a marriage with her handsome cousin.

After he had married Erda, Martha had looked sadly out toward the groves of olive trees, knowing that he was still working with the men, but that he would go home to a new wife. She would not be his. And while she silently attempted to mend her broken heart, she thought of other men who might be working in those groves—men who would hear of her virtue and ask her brother for her hand in marriage.

But that had not happened either. Years had passed. Wet season turned to dry season and back again to wet. Martha had grown older until she had to accept that her age was against her. She was too old to be a desirable bride. Somehow she had slipped into those dangerous years of "old maid."

Yet still she had hoped. Perhaps a widower would notice her. Although it was evil to wish for another woman's death so that she could have her husband, it was really Martha's last chance. Until one day her brother had told her about Jebuseh.

Now, her uncle had snatched even the chance of being a second wife from her. And Martha stared out toward the olive groves and felt very much alone.

God, why has this happened to me? I have worked hard and done my duty. I have taken care of my family and acted appropriately always! I have done everything a woman should do, yet I am passed over!

"Martha?"

She turned to see her brother standing awkwardly behind her, his eyes filled with sadness and guilt. As he shuffled his feet he looked down like the boy that she remembered from so many years ago. With a sigh he rubbed a hand across his eyes.

"I'm sorry," he began. "I don't know what happened. Jebuseh seemed ready to make the agreement final. He seemed ready . . ."

"It isn't you, Lazarus," she said softly. "You did your best."

"I didn't do enough!" Anger singed his words.

"It was Uncle Simon. He hates me."

For once Lazarus was silent and did not defend the old man. He just looked at his sister with a sad smile.

"I'm sorry I married before you," he said, repeating his old regret. "I'm sorry that the men of this village are blind to your goodness. Because I know how good you are, Martha! I know what a kind, hardworking, generous woman you are. I know you."

"A brother always sees more than a husband anyway." She forced a smile.

"Is it selfish of me to be happy that I won't lose you from my house?"

"Yes," she said simply, but she gave him a tender smile.

"Maybe it is," he sighed, shaking his head.

The sound of happy, exuberant voices floated from the house, and Martha was silent for a few moments listening to them. Mahzala would be accepting congratulations right now. Her brothers and father would be proud while her mother would be tearful, despondent at losing her daughter but happy for the girl's good fortune. People would already be thinking of wedding presents and planning what to give the new couple. This was Mahzala's day.

"I always thought you were the prettiest, you know," Lazarus said.

Martha gave her brother an incredulous look. "I may be sad, but I don't need to be lied to."

"I'm not lying. Ever since I was a boy I've looked up to you. You were always so strong and reliable—so much like Mother used to be."

Like her mother? Yes, Martha had much of their mother in her. But their mother had softer features and silky hair and had looked more like Mary, even if Mary had been so unlike their mother in temperament and personality.

"Mother and Mary looked alike," Martha said quietly.

"You and Mother were alike in the ways that matter. Perhaps if they had lived, things would have turned out differently."

"It's no point wondering what if. What's happened cannot be undone."

No, nothing could be undone now. Too many things had happened. Too much sand had been blown away ever to recover one grain again.

Martha had failed as a woman. That much was obvious. A successful woman married and had children. She received respect for her ability to care for her family. What family did Martha care for? Her brother? He was married and had a wife to look after him. His sister's presence only hindered the girl from learning her role properly. Rachel would get along just fine without her. No, Lazarus did not really need Martha—she was simply making herself useful. The truth stung.

But Mary did need her. In a strange way, her sister needed her to buffer her from the village scorn. Martha's appropriate behavior and correct deeds stood like a wall in front of her sister's strange ways. But she did not want to care for Mary. Mary didn't have to be so needy. She could duck her head like the bad woman she was, and accept the cold shoulder of the village without complaint. Actually, she was lucky to be alive! Instead, Mary kept declaring that she had value . . . that she was loved. And where did her value come from if not from the village? Mary had thrown her own value away, and there was no getting it back again. So if she had ruined herself, why did Martha always feel so responsible?

"Do you remember when Mary was only a little girl?" Martha asked suddenly.

"With those big eyes and the mouth so wide you could see her molars when she smiled?" Lazarus said with a chuckle.

"She was different then. Mary didn't have to become what she did."

"It was a long time ago." Lazarus stared across the olive groves at the hazy line of the horizon.

"Sometimes I think that if I'd done my duty, brother," Martha said, her voice tight. "If I'd done what I should have, she would be happily married right now with children and in-laws to frustrate her."

"Everyone chooses their path." He shook his head. "Even Mary."

But Lazarus did not know all the story. He did not know that Simon had slept with his sister since she was a child, shattering the child's trust in adults and life. Nor did he know that Martha had been aware of the situation . . . and had not been able to stop it.

"We all had a hard life," Lazarus said. "Mother and Father died when we were still really little more than children. I had to provide for two older sisters before I could even grow a beard! I had to become a man in my heart before I was one in body. I have often blamed myself for Mary too."

"You?" Martha asked, surprised. "You blame yourself for everything, brother, but to blame yourself for Mary is going too far!"

"I was supposed to act in the place of Father! I was supposed to protect her and watch her. As the man, I was supposed to be vigilant and guard her innocence. I failed. I did not see anything in front of my face. I regarded her with the reverence of an older sister, a woman superior to me and good in every way. I leaned on her instead of using my strength to allow her to rest on me."

"Then we both blame ourselves," Martha said wryly. With a sigh she looked down at the rocky ground.

It seemed the only one not to blame herself was Mary! Their sister had somehow let go of it all. Finding acceptance in Jesus, she forgot about the opinion of the village. But that was selfish of her! Martha could not forget the village. She had to live in it—had to face the shame that Mary had daily brought on their family! Had to face the life of a spinster with no husband, children, or honor because of her sister's sins. And yet Mary did not carry around any guilt with her. She simply approached the world in her usual peculiar manner.

If anyone should shoulder the blame, it was Mary. And if anyone should be crushed under a load of guilt, it should be her. Martha had not gone out to the street. After all, she had had the same parents, same upbringing. Mary should have been stronger. The load was too heavy for Martha. The guilt, multiplied through the years, was bending her back and stealing her future. Yet Mary stood straight and faced the village with her usual defiance.

"I was forgiven!" she kept saying.

But what about Martha?

Who will forgive me?

Martha leaned against her brother's strong arm and felt tears pricking her eyes as she gazed across the ridge of hills that rose between them and Jerusalem. It was the same beautiful sight that she had looked at her entire life. They were the same gray-green olive groves and the same meandering paths. The hills were timeless, and the sun rose and set as it always had.

"Well, brother," Martha said, a matter-of-fact tone entering her voice. "Enough time spent on useless regrets. We have a good face to put forward. There will be a marriage, and we must pretend that this is good news."

"It is, sister," Lazarus said with a sad smile. "You are too good to be the second wife. It was wrong of me even to suggest it."

In the distance she could see Karlan the Cripple slowly heading down the Jericho road. No, not a cripple any longer. She kept forgetting that. But a village remembers. He was tall, taller than one would have imagined before he stood up. His curly black hair hung in glossy waves over his forehead, but today he walked like a man carrying a load on his shoulders. His shoulders—they were strong too. With a sudden blush she realized that he was a handsome man.

"Well . . ." Martha turned back toward the house, pulling her veil up to cover her reddened cheeks.

"I'll take care of you," Lazarus said.

"Perhaps I should go visit Aunt Anna and see if our uncle knows anyone," she said, a twinkle coming into her eye.

He laughed, and they headed toward the house together.

A brother, Martha realized in that moment, was a greater support than a husband with two wives could ever be. Perhaps it could be a comfort to her.

Karlan the Cripple walked slowly back toward his humble home. Of course, he was no longer a cripple, but the cripple he had been seemed to be what everyone saw. A village's memory was stronger than its eyesight.

With his quiet, calm ways he'd worked hard to bring himself up in the world. His distant cousin, Timon, had not had any children. In fact, he had never married. Not many men ever did that. But Timon had left a small vineyard to him when he had died some months earlier. It was more than he could have ever hoped for!

Almost.

Evening approached, and the sun hung low in the sky.

He had prayed for her—had prayed for her one day when he was still only in his teens, begging on the streets of Bethany. He had seen

Martha with some other girls, and he had fallen in love with her then. But falling in love is easier than marrying the girl. Who marries a cripple? A cripple cannot work to provide for his family—cannot keep a wife. A cripple is . . . a beggar. A nobody.

But he'd prayed for her, nonetheless—prayed that God would give him Martha. He would love and respect and be good to her.

And several years later God had even sent Jesus to heal him—to take him by the arm and help him to his feet. Even now he could still remember that tingling feeling as his legs suddenly plumped and grew strong and straight all in a moment. The first wobbling steps of his life were still as clear in his mind as if they had been just moments before.

I'll work! he told himself then. *I'll work, and make up for lost time!*

After he was healed and well, Karlan's distant cousin Timon had allowed him to work his vineyards with him. Still, he did not have anything of his own to allow him to marry. No land, home, or inheritance. So marriage was not possible . . . not yet. But he would work hard to build himself up. And Karlan vowed that he would never beg again.

Jesus had given him self-respect and the worth of a man. And now that God had made it possible for him to inherit a small vineyard he finally had the financial stability required to start a family of his own—Martha was to belong to another.

Jebuseh was well respected and honest. He would give Martha a good life, would he not?

The thought stirred anger inside his chest, and Karlan clenched his fists, the muscles in his arms rippling.

Martha would belong to another. Gossip had already spread the word around town. A village is even worse at keeping secrets than it is at not forgetting! The betrothal was all but finalized. It was better this way for her, he knew. He was not important enough in the community for her family to take notice of him. Her uncle Simon would never countenance an alliance with a cripple.

Was it a boyhood puppy love that he had felt for all these years? Was it something childish that he was refusing to let go of? Perhaps it was. Perhaps Martha had never been God's will for him after all.

146 | MARTHA AND MARY

He allowed his gaze to turn once more toward Martha where she stood with her brother, Lazarus. The sun was shining its low golden rays, enveloping her in a pool of light. Her eyes were laughing, and she stood with a strength he had seldom seen before. She was a woman who had endured—a woman in a million.

And then she looked away, and with her went the golden sunlight.

CHAPTER 18

"Pride goes before destruction."

PROVERBS 16:18

Several weeks had passed since the betrothal of Jebuseh and Mahzala. The family happily planned for the festivities. Jebuseh would not take long to collect his bride, they were sure. He had a full home and household already, so there was little preparation to be done. Rachel was excited about the wedding. She knew that it was a disappointment for Lazarus and Martha, but it was still a wedding—still a celebration! And there would still be a newer wife than she was to join the ranks of the married women. It would elevate Rachel in the village hierarchy, helping to solidify her position. With another woman coming up behind her, she would not have to hold on so tightly to keep from losing her footing. That was how a family worked. Someone behind pushed you forward and nestled you comfortably into place as they joined the group.

Martha would help in the cooking, of course. She knew what was expected of her and always complied. Rachel admired that in her. Strong, Martha always knew the right thing to do and say.

But before the wedding would take place, the family had another dinner to plan for. Jesus, the Healer and the particular friend of Lazarus, had sent word that He would come for a time to rest. And a great dinner was being prepared in the house of Simon in His honor. Jesus had done more for this family than any other they knew of. Healing Simon of leprosy and then raising Lazarus back from the dead, He had given them back their men.

And what was a family without men? Men provided for the women. They took care of the business and arranged for the marriages. A family without its men had to beg for alms on the street. It had no identity.

All of this, of course, had happened before Rachel had married Lazarus. She was a new bride—only four months married. She hadn't ever lived with her husband's sister, Mary, either. Of course, she had heard of her. Who hadn't? But she had somehow believed that when Mary went away that it would be for good and that she would never have to face the humiliation of that woman living in her home.

Rachel must leave soon to help Aunt Yardena with the cooking. Her nausea seemed to have passed for the time being, and she put a hand on her belly, smoothing her fingers over her middle, still flat. Somehow the flatness of her stomach made her feel a little sick again. If she could detect a swelling, she would feel more confident. But there didn't seem to be any difference.

"Have you ever met Jesus before?"

Pulling herself out of her own thoughts, she looked up at Lazarus. "No, husband."

"He is a wonderful man, Rachel," he said, gentle eyes resting on her face. "He is so wise and kind and makes you feel as if you are the most important person on earth."

"Oh, I am too newly married to be of much importance," Rachel said with a blush. "And I would not feel right speaking directly to a man I am not related to."

"It is not the same with Jesus." Lazarus pulled her close to him. "I wouldn't feel dishonored with Him. No, Jesus is the Messiah. Who else could raise the dead?"

Rachel tried to imagine what this strange man looked like, and failed. Everyone spoke so highly of Him. She'd heard of His miracles. And soon she would see Him in the flesh! It was exciting. Her mother and sisters would be thrilled to hear her stories about serving at a dinner at which the healer had eaten.

"Why hasn't He overthrown the Romans yet?" she asked suddenly.

"H'mm?"

"The Romans," she repeated. "Why hasn't Jesus overthrown them yet if He is the Messiah?"

"I don't know," Lazarus said quietly. "I don't know. Perhaps His purpose is deeper than that somehow."

"The Romans are the worst animals ever to subdue us," Rachel said, shaking her head against his shoulder. "I can't see anything more important than ridding us of them. We are God's people, and we should live in honor, not in slavery to beasts."

"I know. But don't speak of such things. You never know who is spying for the Romans, filling their purses by passing along stories. You don't understand the ways of the world, Rachel."

She had said too much! A woman didn't involve herself in politics. She cared for her family. Now Rachel had broken the first rule that her mother had given her before her marriage: *Think only of your family. And if your thoughts stray, never betray them to your husband, lest he think you are not womanly enough.* Mentally she chastised herself for her stupidity. It was better to keep quiet than to let her mouth go. A woman was discreet and never revealed anything unnecessary. Rachel felt like a child again!

"I've missed my friend," Lazarus said after a few moments. "I haven't seen Him for some time. Before I married, I followed Him beyond Jerusalem to hear Him speak. But now I have responsibilities at home."

His wife was silent.

"And we will see Him tomorrow!" he said, giving her shoulder a final squeeze and releasing her. "I'm glad!"

She smiled back at her husband as his face broke into a large grin. There must be something special about Jesus to make her serious husband laugh like a boy. She wondered what it was.

Simon adjusted his robe around his belly. He had lost weight with this sickness, and his appetite still had not returned properly.

His strength was not what it used to be. But he was recovering, and that was something to be thankful for. Although he'd thought he would die, he hadn't. Yes, that was definitely something, wasn't it?

Pouring a dribble of oil into his creased palm, he rubbed his hands together before smoothing them over his gray hair and beard. He would look his best, even if not his strongest. It wasn't as if his wife could stop him from attending a dinner he was throwing, but he wanted to show everyone that he was not an old man yet. Simon was still virile and a force to contend with.

Readjusting his robe, he stepped outside into the blinding sunlight. He hadn't been out of his house in weeks. As he stood in the heat of the midmorning sun he let it flood over him like a welcome bath. Nodding a greeting to a friend who called out to him, he tried to stand taller, afraid that he might appear to be stooping. Later he would stop and talk to his friends and acquaintances, but first he had something on his mind.

When he saw Lazarus coming up the road, Simon waited for his nephew. He had sent for him.

"Uncle!" Lazarus called, a broad smile on his face. "You look as healthy as a young ram!"

Suppressing a smile, Simon nodded. The younger man had always been his favorite nephew. "God be with you, Lazarus," he said, beginning to walk slowly. "I have something to speak with you about."

"And God be with you, Uncle," Lazarus said, sobering.

"This dinner. It is important. Very important."

"I understand." Lazarus nodded. "Jesus is always an important guest, to be sure."

"This dinner will show this village just what our family is made of! I don't need to remind you of the shame we have suffered with your sister's downfall."

Lazarus blushed, and his jaw clenched noticeably. "No reminders necessary," he said in an even voice.

"There will be important men coming from as far as Jerusalem. This meal is not an occasion to air our dirty laundry, if you understand what I am getting at."

"I have never been one to speak out of turn, Uncle."

Simon sighed. So stupid and young! Why couldn't the boy catch a hint when it was thrown directly at him? Was he forcing him to say it in so many words? "I am speaking of your sister." Annoyance edged his words.

"I have two, sir."

"Mary," Simon snapped. "For the sake of all that is good, boy, why must you be so obtuse?"

"You want me to speak with her?"

"It would be a first step," the older man replied, shaking his head. "I want you to keep her away from the feast. I want it to be the way it was when she was sent away. I want no reminders of our past shame to be hiding in my kitchen and touching the food we will be eating. There are Pharisees present who turn their faces from looking at any woman, let alone a woman like her! We have the sensibilities of our guests to consider."

Lazarus did not say anything, and Simon glanced at him out of the corner of his eye. The young man looked worried. His brow was furrowed, and his dark eyes were focused on the dusty ground in front of him. Lips pressed together into a thin line, he seemed lost in his own thoughts.

"Do I make myself clear?"

"Yes, Uncle," Lazarus said, looking up suddenly. "Perfectly clear."

Simon gave a final dismissive nod, then watched his nephew walk away. Too soft, that was the boy's problem. Lazarus had never fully become a man. He was always too concerned about the feelings of women, as if they mattered at all. A woman had a veil for a reason, didn't she? Her feelings belonged behind that veil, where a man didn't need to trip over them. Lazarus would do well to learn how to ignore the pathetic nattering of women and attend to the concerns of men.

And this dinner was one of Simon's concerns. It must go properly, bringing honor to the family and showing the village just what he and his house were . . . And it couldn't be ruined by the presence of the wrong woman!

CHAPTER 19

"A good name is better than fine perfume."

"Serve the wine, Erda," Aunt Yardena said tersely. "And don't spill!"

Erda picked up the jug of fresh wine and slipped away. The men's voices swelled with laughter at a story that Uncle Simon was telling. Martha looked around the corner, watching as Erda poured out the wine, keeping her head bowed down politely. Her veil was raised, and it obscured nearly all of her face. This was not an ordinary dinner party. Because those attending it were important men, discretion was a must. It would not be polite to disturb them while they ate. A good woman only served and backed away again, so that she was hardly noticed.

"Where is Mary?" Yardena whispered, and Martha jumped, not realizing her aunt had been standing so close to her elbow.

"I'm not sure, Aunt. At home, I believe."

Yardena's hair was frizzy from the steam of cooking food, and her cheeks were flushed. Her sleeves were pulled back, baring her plump arms that were now planted firmly on her hips. "She'd better not ruin this." Warning edged her voice.

Martha didn't answer. Who was to say what her sister would do? Mary didn't behave according to expected social rules. Either she didn't think they applied to her any longer, or she didn't care that they did. So how could Martha possibly know what she might do?

"Stupid girl," Yardena muttered. "And she'll ruin your chances, too, you know! Whatever is left of them."

Martha glanced quickly at her aunt. Yes, Mary had ruined more than Martha's chances at an honorable marriage. The woman might be an embarrassment to her aunt, but the disgrace was sharper still when Mary was your sister.

"She'll stay home," Martha finally said, trying to keep the bitterness from her voice.

Yardena sniffed again, jerking irritably at her sleeves that were beginning to slip.

Dinner parties were all-important. They represented honor and status. When a man of high status threw a huge dinner party and you received an invitation, it indicated something about your own status. But even more significant, a host defined himself by his dinners, and guests defined themselves by their position at the table. A well-respected man giving a dinner would assign seats to each of his guests. The closer to the head of the table, the more important the person. That man's perception of each individual's significance spoke volumes. A dinner party was always infinitely more than mere food or company. And behind every successful host there was a kitchenful of women doing the cooking.

Of course, for Uncle Simon's dinner party, Aunt Yardena had charge of the cooking, but every female family member beneath her came to help for the event. It was a large gathering . . . more than 25 men to be fed around the low table. And one of the main guests was the Healer, Jesus. He had brought some of His closest friends with Him.

While it might be an important dinner for Simon, Martha felt the significance of the day as well. Jesus was their personal friend. In the past He had personally complimented her on her cooking. Her flatbread, He had told her, was second to none. As were her stewed lentils and sticky honey bread. She hoped as hard as she could that her sister would obey their uncle's order and stay away from the house as well. Mary's strange, overflowing emotions must not be allowed to ruin the occasion.

"Why is Jesus sitting in the second place of honor?" Erda whispered as she returned.

"The second place?"

The women all peered around the corner, straining to see through the dim lighting. Oil lamps flickered and wavered, throwing their light across the walls, but shadows sometimes obscured faces, and they had to concentrate to be sure from their position. The men reclined around the low table, supported by cushions on the floor. Some of Jesus' friends who had come with Him sat away from the table, as there was no more room. They had pillows, however, and still were comfortable enough. It was true, though. Jesus was sitting two places away from Uncle Simon, and the women looked at each other with raised eyebrows. Had Simon's illness made him forgetful? Was he really recovered?

"Simon knows best," Yardena said crisply. "Wipe those looks from your faces, girls!"

"Rueben of Jerusalem has the place of honor," Martha said. It wasn't right. The feast had been in Jesus' honor. Lazarus had sent the message to invite Jesus, and this would reflect badly on them.

"Rueben of Jerusalem is a very powerful man, my dear," Yardena said softly. "He is also very wealthy. Coming to this feast, could he expect to have anything less?"

"The Messiah is of a higher standing than a rich Pharisee."

"That is still in debate." A tartness had crept into Yardena's voice.

Martha let the subject drop. Convincing her aunt of the social blunder would not solve it. The decision belonged to her uncle, whether he was weak from his past sickness or not. And it was true—many of the Pharisees were not convinced that Jesus was the Messiah. Miracles or not, they had studied the scriptural accounts of the Messiah's arrival, and He was meant to come as a king. Yet who but the Messiah could raise the dead? Still, regardless of her personal experience with Jesus, Martha had to admit that He was not what had been expected. The debate was endless, and sometimes it became quite vicious.

Edging toward the door leading into where the men were eating, she peeked in. Jesus was bending to scoop up some of Martha's own stewed lentils, and she felt a little thrill of pride. Jesus had always said that her lentils were His favorite! It was nice to see that He hadn't been simply being polite when He said it. Uncle Simon looked pale. Obviously he was still recovering from his illness and hadn't regained his full strength yet.

It was then that Martha spotted her. As Yardena and the other women turned back into the courtyard, Martha saw her sister creep into the room where the men were eating. Mary glanced around, was not noticed, and settled herself in the corner next to a servant who was dozing at her post.

Jumbled thoughts raced through Martha's mind. Was Mary coming to disrupt the meal? Did Uncle Simon see her? Aunt Yardena would be furious! The important men would not understand! How many of those men had hired Mary for her services? And mixed in with everything else were feelings of both dread and responsibility. Mary was her sister—somehow, Martha had to fix this. As always, she had to solve it when Mary brought the family shame . . .

Turning away from the door, Martha avoided her aunt's curious look.

"What happened to you?" Yardena asked. "You look as if you have just taken sick!"

"No, Aunt, I'm fine!" Martha tried to sound normal. She slipped back to her post of baking flatbread.

Yardena shook her head in obvious exasperation. It was an important meal, and Martha knew her aunt was under a great deal of pressure to make it come off without a hitch.

Martha's hands moved without her guidance. They knew the work. As for her mind, it was reeling. What would she do? What *could* she do? She couldn't very well enter the room where the men were eating and drag her sister out by her ear. But she had to do something! The thought of Simon being shamed did not bother her. Her uncle deserved it! But that shame would fall on all of them, tainting the whole family ever further. They would all have to carry it, and Mary would be oblivious to the burden.

"Something is wrong with this stew!" Erda exclaimed, sniffing at the pot. Martha could smell it too . . . a strange aroma mixed with the aroma of boiling meat. The cooking spices were strong, but there was something definitely wrong with the scent. Could the meat be rancid?

"What have you done?" Yardena hissed. She dashed to the pot and leaned over it, inhaling deeply. Then frowning, she took a step back and inhaled again. After another step back she sniffed once more.

They all seemed to realize at once that the smell was not emanating from the simmering pot. Their eyes followed Aunt Yardena as the older woman sought the source of the powerful scent. Martha pulled a circle of flatbread, half cooked and still doughy, from the coals, and went after her aunt. Aunt Yardena's hands, spotted with age, Martha realized only now, clutched the edge of the doorway with a white-knuckled grip.

Martha recognized the smell now. It had grown even stronger, wafting in fragrant waves—the scent of a very expensive perfume. Only the wealthiest women could afford it, and even they wore it sparingly! Who could be wearing such an expensive scent? Women were not part of this dinner! No women should be in the room except servants . . . and Mary . . .

It was worse than Martha had thought—so much worse that it made her head suddenly feel light and empty. Remembering it even years later, she would find her stomach heaving with the shock of such impropriety.

As Martha stared, there, kneeling on the ground, crouched down with her veil slipped down into a wrinkled heap on the floor beside her, was Mary. It took several long moments to realize exactly what she was doing. She was pouring perfume on Jesus' feet!

The whole thing was so appalling that Martha wanted to sink into the ground. Her head bare like a harlot, Mary was kissing the feet of the honored guest. So brazen! It wasn't even the kind of scene one expected to see in a bedroom! As she kissed His feet, Mary cried and wiped His ankles dry again with her hair . . . her flowing, sensual hair.

"Oh . . ." Martha moaned. "Oh . . ."

Nothing else would come out of her mouth, and she felt her shock giving way to pure fury.

Jesus was the honored guest! Mary was exposing her hair like a harlot and acting like a madwoman in front of a houseful of influential people—half of whom had probably hired her for her services! Had her sister been within arm's length, she would have slapped her soundly.

"I will stone her myself!" Yardena said, her voice low and dangerous. "Give me something heavy!"

Erda pulled her mother-in-law back. "Don't make it worse, Mother," she pleaded. "Your husband will deal with it! Don't make it worse! A woman of your standing does not fight in front of men. You are higher than that whore is. Show it! Stay calm!"

Martha crossed her arms and clenched her hands into fists, unable to tear herself away from the scene before her. The table had erupted into gasps and horrified whispers. Simon had risen shakily to his feet and was staring at his niece with an expression of disgust that bordered on physical nausea. Then his glance moved smoothly toward Jesus, and he watched the spectacle in silence, his lips quivering in rage, as if he wanted to say something but his voice would not allow him.

"What a waste of money," Martha heard one man say, and she had to agree. Where her sister had gotten such an expensive item, she did not know, but to waste it like that . . . Had it been a gift from a past lover?

"Simon"—Jesus' voice was quiet, but held strange authority—"I have a story for you."

Mary, still bent over His feet, didn't rise, but Martha could sense her sister's body tense. One ear poked out from Mary's hair, and it was pink. She was embarrassed. As well she should be! But still, Martha couldn't help feeling an inexplicable torrent of sympathy for her sister. Somehow Mary had decided that she needed to do it, and now that she had committed herself to it, she was caught as a public spectacle, acting like a crazy woman. After all she'd done to try to recover some remnant of dignity . . .

"There was a man who was very wealthy," Jesus said, leaning back in the way He always did when He told stories. "He was kind, however, and he would lend his money to those less fortunate. Two men came to him for money. One borrowed 500 denarii. The other, a very poor man, asked for only 50 denarii. Both were completely unable to repay, so the wealthy man forgave both debts. Now, which one do you think loved him more?"

Silence reigned. Mary's sniffles could be heard clearly, although she was obviously trying to stifle any sound that she might make.

"The one who was forgiven more, I suppose," Simon said after a moment's thought, frowning.

"True enough. I've seen how you are looking at her. You think that she embarrasses herself. That I don't know about her history."

His gaze was directly on His host now. Appearing uncomfortable, Simon sat back down.

"I do know her history," Jesus continued. "All of it."

Simon stiffened.

"And while you did not do your duty as host and offer to wash My feet from the dust of My journey, she has washed them with her tears. You did not honor Me by kissing Me when I came into your home, but she has not stopped kissing My feet. I have been telling you this evening that I will die, and she is preparing me for My burial." Bending, He gently lifted Mary from her prostrate position.

"This woman," Jesus said, His voice becoming gentle. "Her sins might be many, but they are forgiven. And because she had many sins, she loves Me a great deal. It appears that you, Simon, do not love Me as much."

A momentary silence shrouded the table, then whispering erupted. Jesus seemed to ignore it.

"You are forgiven, Mary," Jesus said. "Thank you for your kindness to Me. Everywhere My story is told, you will never be forgotten for what you have done."

It was a slap in the face of the host. Simon's dinner would not be remembered, but the strange affection of a prostitute instead . . .

The scent of the perfume crept silently through the room, clinging to clothing and nestling into hair.

And Martha could only think, *He knows!* At last someone knew the truth of Uncle Simon and what he had done to the girls in his charge. And with the flooding, choking scent of perfume, she felt a certain elation.

Then a sudden thought occurred to her—if Jesus knew it all, He also knew her failure. Martha hadn't protected her stick-thin little sister with the mouth too large for her face and the peering, trusting eyes . . . she had let her down. She hadn't stopped the bad things from happening to her. As her older sister, it was her role to protect the younger children! It was her responsibility, and she had failed. What Mary became . . . the humiliation brought onto their family . . . it was her fault. Somehow she should have done more, shouldn't have shut her eyes.

The guilt did not leave her for the rest of the evening, even as Martha continued to serve. Cooking and wiping up spilled stew and sweeping the dusting of flour that covered the floor, she did her duty as a woman and as a niece. And the guilt crushed her.

Jesus was about to leave, and goodbyes were being said. Martha stopped short. She wanted to go out to Him, wanted to say that she was sorry for her sister's behavior. But something stopped her. Maybe it was better not to draw any more attention to what had happened, she told herself. Mary had been embarrassed enough for one day.

But the truth was that Martha didn't want attention drawn to herself. Jesus could see too much. Some things she wanted to stay hidden.

CHAPTER 20

"For with much wisdom comes much sorrow; the more knowledge, the more grief."

ECCLESIASTES 1:18

Protecting a sister is exhausting, especially when she does not see its need. Martha had been protecting her sister for years now, but her best efforts never seemed to be enough. No matter what she did, it had never been enough to preserve even the remnants of family honor.

Too much had happened in the past few weeks. It had started out like mere pebbles in her life, then had grown to sizable stones. Now it felt as if the final blow were coming—the giant rock heaved above someone's shoulders and aimed directly at her head.

Martha stood outside her home, staring down the dusty road that led toward Jerusalem. The wind was picking up again, and she pulled her veil around her head, feeling the grit and sand blowing into her hair despite her efforts. But she would not go inside. She wanted solitude, as strange as an ordinary person would find that.

Solitude. Who wanted it? Such a thing was of no use to anyone. People dreaded it. Family was what a person longed for—family held you in place, gave you a sense of belonging. And it provided your life with meaning, didn't it? It was your relationship to others that brought security and honor.

But Martha's relationship to others had brought her the most pain. With a wealthy Pharisee uncle, who could complain? With a kind and loving brother to protect you, who could feel empty? With women in the community nodding their approval when they spoke of your hard work and good cooking, who would not feel fulfilled?

But Martha knew the secret sins of her uncle. And she had not stopped them. Although she had spoken to her sister from time to time, that was all. She had closed her eyes, imagining that her uncle's lecherous violations had stopped. It was easier that way, wasn't it? Easier than opening her eyes and accepting the fact that her uncle was sleeping with her sister and destroying her as surely as if he'd strangled her slowly. But Martha was the good girl who would never speak out of turn or dishonor her family. No, she simply watched as her sister's innocence was stolen from her. That was what a good girl did.

And Martha knew the public sins of her sister. Who didn't? Surely stories still flooded the village and were told around fires late at night that Martha had not yet heard. But the village did have some sense of decency. They wouldn't tell the family the most horrible tales. Those they spread behind your back. And those public sins were so widely known that her sister could not scrub the stain from her robes. It was obvious that Mary would be discredited and shunned. Of course! If Martha could ever drain the love from her heart, she would do the same. She knew the villagers wondered that if one sister could go so bad . . . had such sin lying sleeping inside of her . . . what of the other? Sometimes sin hid longer in one person than another. But a family shared blood and sin . . . and shame. Martha was not safe to marry.

Yet marriage was not impossible! It was still attainable. Jebuseh's interest in her had demonstrated that. Surely it could happen again. But with an uncle like Simon, a man who wanted nothing more in his wicked life than to see Martha ruined, was it really so possible? Other men might become widowers and look about themselves for a new wife. Such things did occur. But Simon, an influential man, would stop every hope she might ever have.

Why could he not have died? Why did he have to recover and continue to plague the family who relied on him?

No, she could not say she was entirely disappointed that she would not marry Jebuseh. An old man, already married, he was not what she had hoped for all these years. But he would have sufficed.

She had pined for her cousin. And what would it have been like to be married to him? Would she be happy? Would she know that her husband was cheating on her? If she did, would it hurt very much? Or would the children be enough for her?

If she was as simple and easy to please as Rachel, perhaps such a marriage would have brought her contentment and satisfaction. But Martha was not so easy to please. Something empty inside of her refused to be filled with anything. Perhaps Rachel was right. Perhaps Martha never would be happy.

"Martha!" her sister-in-law called from inside. "Martha!"

She did not answer.

Life, it seemed, was an endless effort to avoid the flying stones, an anxious attempt to nurse bruises while watching out for other dangers. An emptiness inside her heart that would not fill no matter how she tried.

Everything that should be pure and good was not. An uncle was a predator. An honorable dinner turned into a family shame. A marriage betrothal was nothing but a humiliation. A harlot felt peace, even when rejected by her entire family. And the good daughter felt misery even while doing everything properly.

"Martha!" Rachel exclaimed, flinging the door open to stare at her. "Didn't you hear me?"

Turning toward her sister-in-law, she forced a smile on her face. This was what was expected, wasn't it? What the good daughter did? She smiled. Worked in the kitchen. Did her duty. Carried the family shame on her shoulders. And accepted her old maid status the way a soldier does his death.

"I'm sorry, Rachel. Do you need me in the kitchen?"

"No one makes stewed lentils the way you do, Martha. How could I not need you?"

Although she followed the younger woman inside the house, her heart remained outside, looking down the road, looking and waiting . . . for what? She didn't know. For her future, perhaps? Hope of some sort? Something the perfect shape and size to fit into the hole inside of her heart that throbbed and ached so constantly?

But inside the kitchen, Martha cooked, and her hands worked, and her lips wore the appropriate expression of efficiency and complacency. From time to time Rachel glanced up to smile at the older woman. Her sister-in-law, Martha could see, was comforted.

Rachel hummed happily to herself. Her belly had begun to swell ever so slightly, as if overnight, and she liked the feeling of bending, because it reminded her of the changes in her body. When could she tell people? Soon? Uncle Simon would be pleased. He would celebrate! Aunt Yardena might even feel pride that her nephew had fathered a child within her!

She looked up at Martha, who was expertly chopping onions and garlic, her hands moving in rhythmic grace. Martha seemed to be back to herself again—contented and strong. One could always count on her to be the rock. Although she wore a veil to cover her hair, her expressions needed no hiding. Martha was admirable in every way.

The baby . . . it would be a boy. She just knew it! Even though Uncle Simon longed for girls, Rachel was sure it would be a boy. And they would name him Simon, after his uncle. And little Simon would be a Pharisee like his uncle. He would be descended of the prophets, with the blood of a long lineage of holy men flowing through his veins.

Lazarus had been whispering late at night that he liked the name Moseh, after his father. Rachel had not known Lazarus' father. She knew only Uncle Simon. But somehow, for some unknown reason, Lazarus did not seem to want to name his son after Simon any longer. He wanted to call him after Moseh, his father, instead.

Why would her husband change his mind? Why did he seem disinclined to speak of his uncle? And why did he no longer praise the man for his righteous acts and good work?

But men were emotional and fickle. A woman was the one to be relied on. She kept the home. If a man was its head, a woman was the neck, was she not? Turning him as she wished, she let him think it was his idea. And her baby would not be born for several months yet.

She wondered when she would feel the child begin to move. Her mother would tell her. Her mother would be happy. And her mother would not forbid her to speak of it!

"Martha."

"Yes, sister?"

"Lazarus has agreed to allow me to visit my family," Rachel said, feeling her face glow with happiness.

"That's good. Your family will always be your strongest support."

"H'mm." Rachel leaned her weight into the dough she kneaded, and smiled happily to herself. She had so much to tell her mother—and to ask her! And she would not be returning home a failure, a fruitless tree.

Rachel would be returning home a pregnant woman.

Yardena stood in her kitchen, staring in the direction of the oven. Her husband was better now. He was not dying, so she would not be a widow. She should be relieved, shouldn't she? But instead she felt anxious.

A dead husband did not take another wife to prove his virility and long life. Nor did a dead husband shout and snap. Instead, a dead husband was a memory and not a present worry.

But Simon was different today. He hadn't shouted at her or insulted her. In fact, he hadn't called for her at all.

Normally, his shouting and berating at least meant he required her to be in the same room as he was. But today he was alone in his sleeping quarters. When she pulled the curtain to it aside, she found him with his prayer shawl up over his head, on his knees. He didn't move.

"Husband?" she'd said softly.

It had been more than an hour now. Simon was a righteous man, but something was wrong. Normally he said his prayers standing, face lifted up to heaven and a look of righteous surety on his face. He didn't pray with his face bent down and hidden. Nor did he pray for so long. And he never passed up an opportunity to shout at his wife.

"Please," he finally said in a choked voice. "I need solitude."

But who needed solitude? Even in his foulest moods, Simon had required someone to vent his bile on. For him to want to be alone was strange. A man surrounded himself with his family to remind him of his honor and his position. His wife represented his place in society, and his children assured him that his name would go on and that the next generation would celebrate his life. Friends and relations showed their unanimous support and approval of him. Why did Simon crave solitude?

And when she crouched at the door, listening, it reminded her of his illness. Perhaps his fever had come back.

"God, O God of Abraham," he murmured. "Forgive me! Forgive me . . . I don't deserve for You to show me Your face again, but I beg of it. Forgive me!"

What did it mean? Did he need forgiveness for a transgressed Sabbath law, or was it something horrible that he was about to do?

She dared not ask. But her eyes were wide with alarm.

CHAPTER 21

"All man's efforts are for his mouth, yet his appetite is never satisfied."

ECCLESIASTES 6:7

Rachel had gone to visit her family, and Martha had to admit that the house felt strangely empty without her. Her brother missed his young bride, and he moped about in the evenings, poking his head out into the kitchen area, only to sigh and wander away again.

Martha had to smile in spite of herself. Men never could hide a passing feeling!

It would not be longer than a week. Then Rachel would be back again. But Lazarus didn't like her absence, even for that short time. So when a few days later he came to Martha and announced that they had a guest, she was relieved that her brother would have something to divert his attention.

"We need a meal, Martha," he said briskly. "And no one can cook up a meal the way you can!"

"Who is our guest?" she asked, peering past him into the living area. But she didn't need an answer. She saw Him, sitting comfortably on a carpet with a pillow under His arm. He looked up and gave her one of His spontaneous smiles.

"Oh, it's Jesus!" she said, the happiness of the moment finally reaching her. It would be a good day! Not every day He came through Bethany and stopped by to eat with His old friends! Part of her had been worried that after that atrocious dinner at Simon's home, the visits might stop.

Quickly Martha looked around, eyeing the contents of pots and mentally measuring herbs. What did she have ingredients for? If she started the honey bread now, it would be done and cooling in time to eat after the meal. The lentils needed to be started. There were fresh cucumbers left, and some dried figs a neighbor had brought by only hours before.

There was nothing like planning a meal to divert her attention from shadowy fears. And there was much to do! If Mary would start on the cucumbers, then work on a fresh batch of bread, Martha could begin the lentils and honey bread, which Jesus had always complimented particularly.

When she looked out into the courtyard, Mary was nowhere to be seen. It was just like her. She avoided the kitchen with the dexterity that a mouse uses to escape a broom.

Well, if she was out of the house, perhaps it was better. Jesus had seen just about enough of her brazen antics! It was time to start covering the embarrassment with proper etiquette once more.

This was what remained for her—kitchen work and entertaining. Such was her life now. It was all she had, and she would do it well. If no children would remember her, at least the village would never see the likes of her cooking again. Mothers would hold her up as an example to their daughters of how a woman should act. She would make up for the stain on the family name, covering up Mary's disgrace.

And maybe . . . dare she think it? Maybe one day a man might want her.

Martha's fingers had already begun their work. She knew what needed to be done, but two more hands were required to do it in a satisfactory period of time. Jesus would be hungry, and it wasn't right to make Him wait all night before He could eat. A proper host could predict her guest's needs and wishes.

Where was Mary? No, it wasn't better for her to stay away. She needed to come to the kitchen like a woman and help with the work!

As her hands automatically performed their work Martha listened to the men's conversation.

"It is much more blessed to be poor, Lazarus," Jesus was saying. "The poor know how much they need God. The rich oftentimes forget Him, believing that money will save them from every harm. But how can it? It is God who clothes the flowers, isn't it? It is He who brings the rain and the sun, who appoints a time to be born and to die. The poor know this, because one day of rain affects the manual worker's income. One poor harvest affects their food supply drastically. If a thief steals their cloak, they don't have another to cover themselves with that night! And for each obstacle in life, they turn to God."

It was true. Martha nodded to herself and turned back to her work. The same could be said for the overlooked woman. Children were security for old age, and without them she would rely on charity or kind nephews. God would have to provide their every need! She would ask Lazarus to repeat everything to her that evening . . . or if it was too late, the next day. Jesus had wisdom that no one else had. He could see the world in a way that society did not notice.

With a sigh she realized that she did not have enough dill. She didn't like to be frugal with her herbs when she cooked. It was a sign of poverty. But the dill would be scant in the cucumbers, and Martha blushed at the thought. Jesus would not say anything, but to have Him notice was bad enough! She had thought to buy more at the market, but she had forgotten when she stopped to look at some fine-quality fabric. Jebuseh's family had made it, and everyone knew that no one wove finer material. She would have worn beautiful garments made of fabric like this . . . perhaps even finer! But those hopes were in the past now. Mahzala would be enjoying those privileges soon enough.

Where was Mary?

"But what of God's blessing on the rich?" Lazarus was asking. "If He blesses the rich, why do you say the poor are blessed?"

It was a good question her brother had asked, one that she had pondered herself. Good for him to have a quick mind! Martha arranged the onion and garlic cloves on the chopping block and wiped a wisp of hair out of her eyes.

"Every good thing comes from God," Jesus replied. "And the rain falls on the wicked and the righteous alike, does it not? Just because a man enjoys God's blessing does not mean he has earned it, or deserves it. In fact, no one deserves any good thing! Humanity is steeped in sin. To mistake wealth for a life that pleases God is wrong. God blessed Abraham with wealth. But was Job less righteous because he lost everything?"

The sound of her chopping drowned out their voices. If she sat listening though the door, she'd never get the meal cooked! A woman's work was endless.

If Mary were here, she would set her to work right away. This was just like her, wasn't it? Always shirking her duty as a woman. Martha looked up at the door anxiously. How long before the woman found her way home again? A better question was How long before her shame stopped draining the happiness from Martha's life?

Finished with the chopping, she scraped the onion into a neat pile, her eyes swimming with water from the odor.

"Lord, why don't You become our king?"

Martha froze. That was Mary's voice! What was she doing there? Wiping her eyes with the corner of her veil, Martha went to the door and looked in. There, next to Lazarus, was Jesus, looking relaxed and happy. And at His feet, her knees tucked up to her chin like a small girl, sat Mary.

Would she never be appropriate? Would she never stop being an embarrassment? Martha sighed, but something inside of her would not back down. This was not fair! All her life she had always done everything right, was the one who always shouldered the responsibility! Although she had never tarnished the family's reputation, she was left paying the price! Expected to whip up a meal at a moment's notice, she found herself alone in the kitchen while Mary sat in the living area like a man!

Of all people, Jesus should see the unfairness of it all! He had seen Mary at her worst, and even forgiven her. But He had also seen how hard Martha had worked, how much of herself she put into her family, how tired she was from all the effort of putting up a good face. Some things were proper, and some were not. This was over the line!

"Lord!" Martha said, frustrated tears choking her voice. "Do you not notice that I am doing all the work? Will you let Mary sit about like a man and make me do everything? Tell her to come help me!"

Jesus looked up, no surprise on His face, and glanced from one sister to the other. Martha stood in the doorway, her face splotchy with anger, her hands balled up into fists. Mary sat, a blush rising in her cheeks and licking her lips uncomfortably from her position on the floor. She shifted, about to get to her feet.

"Martha, Martha," Jesus said. "You worry about a meal and about dill, don't you? You worry about the cooking times and the proper temperature of the oven. You keep worrying. But Mary has chosen something different. She has chosen not to worry, and to learn more about God's kingdom. I can't take that away from her."

Feeling the color drain from her face, and with one veiled look at her sister that promised a tongue-lashing to come, she turned back to the kitchen.

Even though she clamped one onion-scented hand over her mouth and squeezed her eyes shut, the hot tears seeped from under her lashes. It was too much! It was unfair! After all she'd done, after all the work she had put into this family and into their honor, she had embarrassed herself in front of their guest.

Mary could pour perfume on Jesus' head and cry onto His feet with an uncovered head, and Jesus defended her. But when Martha asked for something that was rightfully hers—her sister's help in the kitchen—she was denied it!

This was not the way a fully grown woman acted. She did not cry in her own kitchen! Even when she took several gulping breaths in an attempt to control her tears, the fresh memory of her embarrassment started them again, and she sank down to the floor, trying to stifle any sound she might make.

Just then she heard a sound behind her. It was Mary, she thought. Her sister had come to help after all, just in time to see her sister's humiliation. It was too much!

"Get out, Mary!" she whispered fiercely. "You chose to act like a man, so continue doing so!"

"Oh, Martha . . ."

But the voice was not Mary's. Deep and gentle, it made her want to cry all the harder.

"Lord, I've humiliated myself!" Martha said, turning slowly. "I want to humbly apologize for my behavior. If You desire Mary's company, then I cannot refuse You."

"I desire your company too," He said. "We are friends, aren't we?"

Martha wiped awkwardly at her face, trying to erase the signs of her tears, but she knew that was to no avail. Blushing, she looked around the kitchen area, then back at Jesus.

"Lord, it isn't proper that a man come here," she said a low voice. "No man ever comes into this place."

"Your brother can see Me from the doorway. There is no impropriety."

"It is lowering Yourself, Lord."

"There you are wrong, Martha," He said with a laugh. "It is a social peculiarity, yes, but it does not lower My honor in any way."

He bent and picked up a plate and a cucumber.

"Do I chop it into small pieces?" He asked.

Speechless, Martha stared at Him. He looked back in silence, His eyebrows raised questioningly. Was He testing her?

"When you chop them," He said, rephrasing his question, "do you chop them into small slices?"

"Yes, Lord, I do," she said, waiting for the object lesson.

There was none. Jesus took a knife and began carefully to cut the cucumbers into small slices, focusing on the work in front of Him.

"Oh, Lord, don't!" she gasped. What was this? Why was Jesus disgracing Himself?

"If a man is to do God's will, he must be the servant of all. And who serves more than a woman? It is her life. She is born into the role, and she is taught how to serve from the time she is a small child."

"Yes, Lord, but You are not a woman!"

"No, Martha." Jesus looked directly at her for the first time. "I am a man. But I am willing to serve. This kitchen is yours, and I will not do anything in it that you will not allow Me to do." He put down the knife.

Martha was silent.

"Your heart is broken," He said simply.

She lowered her eyes.

"Your heart broke many, many years ago," He went on. "It broke when you saw what your sister endured at the hands of your uncle, and you have never recovered."

"It was my fault," she said faintly.

"You have endured much. I know all the times you have cried in your life. You were always a strong woman, and tears have meant that you saw no hope at all."

Jesus squatted on the floor.

"Let me tell you a story, Martha. It is one I have told before, but I don't think you have heard it."

"Yes, Lord?"

"A man had two sons. One was young and rebellious. The other was honest and good. The young rebellious son told his father, 'I want my inheritance now, while you are still alive. I don't want to wait till you die! Give it to me, and let me live my life.'

"So the father, heartbroken, did as his son requested, gave him his inheritance, and watched him leave. The good son stayed at home.

"While the younger son spent his life drinking and womanizing, the older son remained with his father, working the fields, organizing the servants, and making sure that his father's lands returned a profit. He put his heart and soul into the land, and he made his father proud.

"One day his younger brother returned home, stinking of pig manure and repentant. The younger son begged his father's forgiveness, which the father readily gave. In fact, the father ordered a large feast to celebrate his son's return!

"How do you think the older son felt?"

How would he feel? He would feel as Martha did! She could see him, an honorable man who had put his life into his family, perhaps even delaying his own marriage to give his father all his strength. She could see him, tall and strong with a proud chin, struggling to control his rage as his younger, irresponsible, weak-willed brother came doggedly back home again. Martha was silent, but after a moment she realized that Jesus was waiting for an answer. How would the brother feel?

"Angry," she said quietly. "Unfairly treated. Why should the father celebrate the younger son when all he did was wrong, and not celebrate the son who had stood by him all those years? He would feel frustrated. Angry. Used."

"Well said," Jesus replied, nodding. "And that is exactly how he felt. He stormed out of the house and refused to go to the feast. His father followed him and said, 'Look, my son, you have been the good son, and everything I have is yours. But your brother was lost to us. Now he is found! Your brother was dead to us—now he is living! Let us celebrate together!'"

As Jesus lapsed into silence, Martha shifted uncomfortably.

"Lord," she said after a moment. "I was the good daughter. I worked for my family and tried to cover the dishonor we endured from my sister's actions. I did things that were expected of me. And now I live with the shame my sister brought on us!"

"You blame your unhappiness on her."

"Yes, I do."

"You believe that if it weren't for her, you would have married already. You would have children of your own."

"Yes."

"And what if it were not her fault at all?"

Horror seeping through her body, Martha froze. It was her worst fear—that the fault did not lie with her sister. Her head began to swim, and she swallowed several times.

"Then I am a less-worthy woman than I believed," she said woodenly.

"You are a good woman, Martha. But you have not trusted God to provide for you. If He provides for the small birds and the wild-flowers and lilies that grow out in the field, He will do the same for you, too! It does not fall to you to correct where your sister has gone wrong. Your responsibility is much different."

"What must I do?"

"Let me finish the story I began. There was something that the older brother failed to do. When his brother left the family house and went out into the world, the older brother got angrier and an-grier, because the younger brother's actions had tarnished his name and his father's name. But while the older brother was angry and correct, his old father was sad and despondent.

"'I miss my son!' the old man cried. 'His mother bore him, and I loved him and cherished him. Now it is like he is dead!'

"'He is dead to us!' the older brother exclaimed. 'I will never forgive him!'

"So he did not go after his brother or try to bring him back home. He had begged him, before he left, to reform his evil ways and to stay at home, but the younger bother would not listen. After the boy had gone, the older brother wished only that he would never return and bring a bad name on the family. So when he saw his brother coming, he did not rush out to greet him or throw his arms around him. Instead he turned his back and nursed his anger."

Martha said nothing.

"You tried to save your sister, Martha, but you gave up. Now that she is reformed and returned home to you, you cannot forgive her. But you cannot change the past. You cannot change her past sins or the village's view of her or your family. In fact, you cannot even change what it has done to your own life. The things that you cannot change, you must leave to God. God can fix them. The things that you can control, however, you must do."

"And what can I control?"

"You can go out to your sister and hold her. You can tell her how you love her. You can welcome her home and let go of your anger. The rest God will take care of."

"It is so hard," she murmured.

"It is. But I must tell you something."

She looked up.

"Your happiness will not come from a husband or children."

Martha frowned. What was this? Of course it would, if the man were the right one!

"Nor will it result from the village's approval of you. Wealth and honor will not bring it. All those things, once achieved, still feel empty."

"Then where will I find happiness?" Martha asked desperately. "Where?"

"From God," Jesus said simply. "From doing His will. From caring for your sister when no one else will. From loving an evil man when he begs your forgiveness, which very soon he will. From making life happier for those around you. By doing this, you are doing God's will, and you will feel His peace and His comfort. Happiness comes from prayer and seeking the presence of My Father."

Martha glanced out the doorway of the courtyard and saw her sister walking slowly away from the house. Her head was down, and her veil covered her hair improperly. One stray curl escaped the side, and she moved with the heavy steps of a woman with a large load to carry. The sun was low in the sky, and her shadow stretched out long behind her.

"She needs you," Jesus said.

Tears clouded Martha's eyes, and she looked for several moments into the kind, dark ones of the man in her kitchen.

"I'm afraid," she whispered.

"I know," He said softly. "You must trust your heart to the One who created it."

As Martha went out into the cool evening, she pulled her veil up over her hair and hurried after her sister. When she caught up to her, she reached out and took her arm. Mary turned toward her, and after a hesitation, Martha put her arms around her sister and held her close. Mary wrapped her own arms around Martha's neck, and after several moments Martha could feel her sister's body begin to shake. It was then that Martha let herself cry, the hot tears soaking into her sister's veil.

"I'm sorry," Martha whispered finally.

"It is I who should be sorry," Mary said. "I'm sorry for what has happened to you because of me. I've not only ruined myself, but you, too. And you were always so good. You deserved better than my fate."

"I didn't protect you! I didn't know how. I wasn't strong enough."

"You couldn't," Mary replied, pulling back to look her sister in the face. "It was too big even for my big sister . . . But the One who could did."

"I hate myself for it," Martha continued, the words rushing out. "I've hated myself all these years. I've blamed you for no man wanting me, but it isn't your fault. I've become bitter—I've become an ugly woman!"

"No! You are not ugly. I remember as a girl thinking that I was hideous and that I deserved Simon's touch. I thought I was ugly, and so when a man wanted me, I lapped it up. All I wanted was for someone to see some beauty in me. If they did, no one ever said so. But I will tell you what I see in you. You are beautiful—you are lovely."

And Martha's eyes welled up with tears again. "No, not like you," she told Mary. "Maybe in reputation, but not in feature, or in my heart."

"Beautiful!" Mary said fervently, fire in her eyes. And she pulled her sister close again.

Several villagers stopped to look at the strange sight of the sisters silhouetted against the setting sun, their arms wrapped around each other. They stood like two lilies, the sun pouring its last molten drops over their forms.

She did not have a husband or children. The family shame remained. But Martha had something she had not had for a long time: a sister, a new beginning, and, most of all, forgiveness. And despite this crazy, out-of-control sensation, she felt safe somehow.

"O God," Martha prayed. "Take care of us!"

The sun was setting on the small village of Bethany, its golden rays slowly slipping behind the Mount of Olives. The village was settling for the evening. Smoke from cooking fires rose in lazy columns into the sky, and the bleat of goats and the laughter of children echoed faintly. In one wealthy home a Pharisee, still weak from a long illness, prayed on his knees while his wife in the kitchen silently worried about his strange behavior. Not far away Lazarus relaxed with his old friend Jesus, feeling the cares of the world evaporating, if only for the brief visit. And outside, two sisters clung to each other as if for dear life.

"Consider the lilies . . ." Jesus was saying, His voice quiet and relaxed. "Not even Solomon in all his splendor could match their beauty. God cares for them, even though they live for a short season and then wither and die. How much more will God care for you?"

POSTLOGUE

The old woman smiled, showing the three teeth remaining in her mouth, and scratched idly at her chin. Hunched over and leaning at an awkward angle on a stick, she hobbled next to another old woman—shorter and darker in complexion, but with the same dusty gray hair. Sisters, living together now that their husbands had died, they'd been known in this village for three generations now.

"I've heard it's final," the first said.

"Eh?" her companion retorted, squinting and bending closer.

"It's final, I said!" She raised her voice.

"Final?" the second asked. "What's final?"

"The betrothal! Martha, poor Moseh's daughter . . . the good one!"

"Ah! The second sister nodded enthusiastically. "The good one . . . to that crippled boy."

"Yes, the crippled boy. Martha's a good girl."

"And what about the other sister?" she asked, cocking her head to one side like a curious bird. "The bad one?"

"Time will tell. Time will tell."

"Old to be getting married, though." Puckering her toothless mouth, she silently told herself, *Thought she'd be an old maid for good, that one!*

"Eh!" The first woman shrugged her shoulders. "What's to be surprised at anymore? Men and women have been doing this since the beginning. It's love, they say."

"Loves her, does he?"

"Since he was a boy, they say. Only a blind old bat like you would miss the way he melted when she came by!"

"Bah!" Her sister waved a weathered old hand and winked with good humor. "They love each other, eh? Love, love . . . Love is a mystery. Leave that one to the God above, I say!"

"You say too many things!"

"Eh?"

"I said, you say . . ."

"Eh?"

"It isn't worth shouting it to the neighbors, you deaf old thing." With a hoarse laugh she shook her old weather-beaten head.

They resumed their hobbling gait down the dusty streets of Bethany.

"Love is a mystery," the second sister repeated, chuckling to herself. "Love comes as natural-like as morning. Just got to wait sometimes, is all. Just got to wait. Leave that one to God above, that's what I say!"

2/7/08

Finish 2/6/08

CAPTIVATING STORIES OF GOD'S LEADING

PATTY FROESE NTIHEMUKA

TRUDY J. MORGAN-COLE

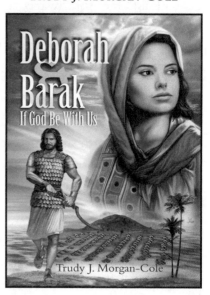

She was a broken, cruel woman. Her heart was numb, and her hope gone—until she met the Man who looked at her with gentle respect in His eyes. This inspiring biblical narrative tells of a woman whose life fully changed after an encounter with the Savior. 978-0-8280-1958-3. Paperback, 160 pages.

She is a prophet. He is a warrior. They have been called to a shared purpose—to help God's people during difficult times. This masterfully written narrative brings to life the biblical account of Deborah and Barak—an amazing story of hope, courage, and God's leading. 0-8280-1841-3. Paperback, 240 pages.